Holiday Hotel

SIMONA ISLAND, BOOK 1

POPPY MINNIX

HOLIDAY HOTEL

POPPY MINNIX

City Owl
Press

This book is a work of fiction. Names, characters, places, and incidents either are products of the author's imagination or are used fictitiously. Any resemblance to actual events or locales or persons, living or dead, is entirely coincidental and not intended by the author.

HOLIDAY HOTEL
Simona Island, Book 1

CITY OWL PRESS
www.cityowlpress.com

All Rights reserved. Except as permitted under the U.S. Copyright Act of 1976, no part of this publication may be reproduced, distributed, or transmitted in any form or by any means, or stored in a database or retrieval system, without the prior consent and permission of the publisher.

Copyright © 2021 by Poppy Minnix.

Cover Design by MiblArt. All stock photos licensed appropriately.

Edited by Mary Cain.

For information on subsidiary rights, please contact the publisher at info@cityowlpress.com.

Print Edition ISBN: 978-1-64898-107-4

Digital Edition ISBN: 978-1-64898-106-7

Printed in the United States of America

*For those who take holidays to the maximum enthusiasm.
Your sparkle is appreciated.*

1

PACK YOUR BAGS, MRS. CLAUS

Whoever invented corset boning is definitely on the naughty list.

This red velvet monstrosity makes breathing problematic, and there's marabou stuck in my lip gloss. But it will all be worth it when James walks down the hall and finds me stretched out on the living room rug.

It's been one month, three weeks, and five days since he's touched me or kissed me or even tried to catch a glimpse of me in the shower. I can't remember the last time we laughed ourselves into a vigorous ab workout or the last time I earned one of his you're-a-goof-but-you're-my-goof grins.

That changes now.

Blowing aside the poofy ball that keeps bombarding my cheek from my Santa hat, I shift in my corset to see which angle is best. On my stomach in a pin-up pose with my ankles in the air and crossed, I think. Good cleavage angle with that one.

The clock I put on the wall yesterday says seven fifty-three, and James will be heading for the front door at eight to run. In this sexy Mrs. Claus getup, with a playful pose with my candy cane rod, I'm going to get us out of this stagnant stage in our relationship. He will love it. I wince and reconsider my hopes. He will pay attention and hopefully remember that he likes my company for more than movies on the couch.

The tight ball in my stomach could be from the steel boning tucked in crimson velvet, but my sweaty palms tell me it's beyond that. I need more fun times and I'm going for it. Besides, Christmas is the ultimate time for antics. It's also a time for decorations, but I'm missing those. With our recent move, that would be too much stress, according to James. That's valid, as I take holiday decor to a ridiculous degree, but I still have antics—my wheelhouse—and it's been a while since I allowed myself to fly free.

We need a push. We've been working nonstop—him at his new location and me on a particularly demanding client—all while unboxing. And we were drifting before the move, existing side by side yet alone. Maybe while making the best of this untypical holiday, I'll start a new tradition. The Mrs. Claus surprise—pre-coffee Cozette laid out on a fuzzy white rug to set the alluring scene, ready for a fun-filled day of sexiness.

Footsteps. He's awake and moving from the bedroom. My heart smashes against the corset's marabou trim. I'm shocked he didn't notice how excited I've been over the last few days. Was this the best idea? I shake that thought away. I think I'm sexy, and so will he. It will be fine. One deep breath and I prop the end of the thick candy cane stick in my mouth, mindful of my bright red lipstick, and throw my shoulders back, displaying my heaving bosom, which I don't need to fake because I'm panic-panting.

"Cozette?" James asks from the hallway. "Why do you have Christmas music playing so loud?" He steps into the living room and keeps going toward the door, eyes on his phone, probably routing his morning run.

"Ahem," I mumble around peppermint.

When he drags his eyes up, they pop in surprise for a split

second, then sink into an expression he aims at me when I've done something out-of-bounds—a blank hazel-eyed stare, plus the slightest nose scrunch.

But no heat.

No interest.

No sexy.

"What are you wearing?" he asks.

My eyes widen. Heat burns my cheeks at this asinine idea. I'm onstage and the one person in the audience, the man who is supposed to love and support me, just discarded his complimentary tickets to this performance.

"You know what? Fa la la you and your little dog too!" I leap up and bite back a hundred angry, hurt words that would only give him more ammunition to judge me. Sorry for trying to have a sexy Saturday before the holidays.

"I-I don't have a dog." He tugs at his winter running shirt and eyes the door to freedom.

I chirp a crazed note of sarcasm. "Well, get one to keep you company, because I'm gone."

Hey, now that follow-up turned out better than expected. One micro-win for me. With a pivot on my shiny red stilettos, I catwalk down the hall. My fast strides send a chill over my bare backside, as the sexy Mrs. Claus skirt I'm wearing isn't exactly full coverage. At least the Santa hat is keeping my head warm.

James used to have fun, used to smile at my shenanigans. He's never been the kind to tackle me, though I'd appreciate that treatment when my lady parts are busting out of a scrap of red velvet and I'm sucking on a candy cane as if it's the best lover I've ever had. Hell, it's the best lover I've had in months.

I'm getting nothin' for Christmas except a Cozette-is-weird face and a *What are you wearing?*

I tug my teal suitcase from the closet shelf and pitch in my clothes from the oak dresser. Everything in our bedroom is beige or wood except for two bright, patterned throw pillows I bought while James was at work. He shoves them in the closet each night, and I toss them on the bed each morning.

"What are you doing?" he asks from the doorway.

"I told you, I'm out, done, finito. It's the motherfrolicking end scene, James."

"Cozette." His tone as he groans my name is an exasperated complaint about my overwhelming nature. Or that's what it sounds like to me. "You need to tone it down. You're upset."

My cheeks heat again. Yes, I am *upset*. I've let this man "tone me down." My style, my language. I've altered everything about me because feelings and bright things make James squirmy.

"How could I let this happen?" I whisper to myself.

"What?"

I move to the closet, jerking everything that's not black or gray off hangers and cramming it all in the suitcase. "We've been together for two years, and I've pushed myself aside to be what you want because I love you."

I'm not feeling the love at the moment, and my heart is racing for freedom instead of embracing my this-relationship-is-over panic. That can't be good.

"Cozette," James grumbles, rubbing his forehead. I wait for him to continue into a reprimand as he always does. Three... two... "That's not—"

There it is.

"No." I slam my suitcase shut, but it won't close all the way. I jab the cascades of unruly fabric inside with my finger. "It is the truth. Somewhere along the line, I forgot about me in this relationship. Today I let myself out, and you don't want me. You want tame and easy and boring. I'm not that person, James. I'm sexy Mrs. Claus, and you're not my Santa."

"This is about sex?" He displays his palms at me, lanky fingers splayed. They haven't been in my vicinity for too long. So long, I'm not sure I want them on me anymore. "I guess it has been a couple of weeks," he says. "Sorry. I'll try to—"

"Hold it right there, Jack Frost." I jerk my bag off the bed, tuck an accent pillow under my arm, and brush by him to head toward the bathroom. "That's the problem. You shouldn't have to try. When it's been over a month, and you walk in the living room to me fellatioing a candy cane while wearing this getup, the obvious path is to replace the peppermint stick with your dick. Your mind didn't even go there."

If our sex life had been a passionate romp long ago, I'd worry about stress from his job or the move, but that's not it. We don't match. Never have, and I'm not sure why I thought a relocation would somehow make things better between us.

"It's fellating. And it's not always about sex, Cozette."

I shove toiletries and makeup into a shoulder bag. "No, it's not. It's about talking, laughing, going out, and making up words like 'fellatioing' because it's more fun to say. We act like we're settled down with kids, but we don't even have pets tethering us to this tiny prison. Is it too difficult to leave the house on a Friday night? Maybe go to a brunch and meet other people our age? You don't want me to explore without you, but you won't leave the apartment. There's a massive city out there, and I've gotten only as far as the coffee shop."

"We've gone farther than that." James tugs at the waistband of his running shorts. "I'd rather stay in. I enjoy our quiet time." His monotone voice grates on the one nerve I have left.

"It's all quiet time!" Except for now, because I'm yelling. "Not to mention, you haven't even attempted to stop me from packing. We're done."

I zip the bag closed, exit the bathroom, and drag the suitcase, my laptop bag, purse, and throw pillow down the hallway, bumping into the wall twice. The stilettos aren't helping my graceful exit.

"What do you want me to do, unpack your stuff?"

"I want you to care," I toss over my shoulder.

At the front door, I eye my corset and gratuitous cleavage. "Ugh." I drop everything to the floor and shuck my shoes.

James steps aside as I pass him on my way back to the bedroom. How can he not get this? Did the hundred times I've asked to go out not give him a clue to my state of mind? I should have gone alone, met some friends or taken on some smaller local projects, but he'd pout if I went exploring without him, and when he went in search of running routes, I had no hope of keeping up with his speedy strides.

I pause in the bedroom and take a cleansing breath. "I want you to show an ounce of emotion that the woman you claim to love is leaving you."

The black sweatpants I left in the drawer are good enough for now. While I think it'd be poetic to walk away dressed as a holiday temptress, it's December in New York. I've had frostbite-free legs for twenty-five years, and I'd like to continue that streak.

"Hey, don't go. We can work this out. The Christmas party is tomorrow."

I stop dead in my tracks. "Oh, is my presence requested at your holiday party? Your boss will not like this breakup one bit, and you know why? Because I'm the only one who talks. I'm entertaining." Regathering my pile of stuff, I head to the door. "At least someone appreciates that."

Stomping my bare feet into my boots, I shove my stilettos into my winter coat pockets, loop my laptop bag and purse over my head, and walk out the door. "I'll pick up the rest of my stuff later."

"Cozette," he says from our apartment door.

The elevator dings. He's not even going to follow? Fully dressed, with no obligations but his self-imposed running time, he stands in the hallway, one foot from the safety of home, watching me walk away.

The stupid part of me that thought he'd simply *try* when

our relationship boiled down to this inevitable moment withers away as the elevator doors shut. Sure, he takes longer to vocalize. Unlike me, he thinks everything through before he speaks, but still. He won't even attempt to convince me to stay?

Leaning against the wall, I wipe away a dumb, hot tear.

Two years of sweet moments had dissolved into bitter boringness.

It's over.

James further dashes my teeny hope of a passionate reunion when I get to the empty lobby. He and I have watched enough romance movies to know that when one person leaves, the other sprints the stairs, or races through the airport, or borrows a flippin' bicycle to cut off their true love's escape.

They do anything to win them back.

But James doesn't burst through the stairwell door, chest heaving and stammering about what a fool he's been. I'm absolutely certain he's already gone back into our apartment.

Oh, he'll consider coming after me, pace the hallway while biting his thumbnail, antsy because he's missing his typical running time. Then, he'll call his twin and they'll chat about how irrational and reckless I am. How my exit is one of my tantrums and I'll return home forthwith. Except they'd never use "forthwith." Too uncommon.

My luggage wheels rattle across beige tile as I roll my suitcase to the door. Outside the glass doors, people pass, bundled up in scarves and hats. The city is a wall of gray stone that blocks out the sky.

I have nowhere to go. We moved three months ago for James's programming career. Since then, I've been working my virtual event planner job from the couch or coffee shop. The closest friends I have are the three baristas on rotation, and only one of them remembers my name. But I do exemplary work when caffeinated and free from beige everything, so that will be my think-this-through spot.

The ding of the elevator makes me jerk to attention. Maybe? Possibly? Could it be?

The doors slide open and a couple hobbles out, bundled up in near-matching gray wool coats. Snowflake-white hair peeks out from under her beret and from his fedora. He leans on a cane, and she leans on him like they're posing for a greeting card geared toward couple goals.

How many times have they broken apart and patched themselves back together? He mumbles something laced with the rasp of decades, and her lips quirk, revealing aged beauty carved from a million laughs.

Past them, the elevator clanks shut. The glowing yellow floor number stays halted on *L*.

James will expect me to come back. It's my M.O. Freak out, cool down, slink home. I'm reliable like that.

Not today.

I swing open the door and slam into an arctic wall of cold. A squeak crosses my lips, promptly freezes, plummets, and shatters on the concrete. Why did I ever agree to move to this popsicle hell?

The hundreds of holiday-decorated windows a few blocks away help thaw me out a little. And it's rumored that I can find any obscure material item in city stores. Oh, the pizza and bagels are so delicious that nowhere else in the world could hope to replicate the taste and texture, but whatever—it's cold.

As I shiver my way to the coffee shop, cars travel the potholed grid like Pac-Man chasing dots while ghosts follow, weaving between each other and popping out of adjoining streets. All I can smell is frozen concrete and exhaust. The dancing neon mug in the window just beyond a wall of steam billowing from a sidewalk grate is a beacon in this gray, frantic world. I take the seat closest to the back to keep away from the frigid whoosh each time someone enters, but it's still freezing. The woman next to me scowls at my haul of bags, and I refrain from flipping her off as I place my throw pillow on the seat to mark it as mine. At the counter, I'm greeted by one of the baristas who doesn't know my name.

Marco is an aspiring actor from Venezuela. He lives in a flat with four other theater friends—one of whom steals all his rice pudding and he is *not* pleased. He spells my name C-O-S-E-T.

The cup of chocolate ganache peppermint espresso with cream and whip warms my hands. After one sweet sip that heats a path to my soul, I declare it the ultimate beverage for a 9:00 a.m. breakup. I fish my phone out of my overstuffed purse. No calls. Fine, then. It looks like I'm headed home for Christmas after all.

I'd told my parents we were staying in New York because of James's new job and the holiday party, but that's not an issue anymore. North Carolina, here I come.

Dad answers on the second ring. "I was about to call you. Hello, daughter of mine from the great big city of New York!" He sings "New York" so loud I have to pull the phone away from my ear and the scowling woman levels up her bitch-face.

When his long note tapers to silence, I tuck the phone back against my ear. "Hello, father of mine, who now gets to spend the holidays with his loving daughter."

"What? Did James get off work for Christmas Eve?"

"No, but we broke up, and now I get to come home for Christmas." I take a deep breath to calm the tightness in my throat. "Yay."

The woman stops scowling and stares into her coffee cup.

"Oh, Cozette. Sorry, sweet pea. Can you work it out? You two have been together a while, and you just moved. It's probably stress."

It's boredom, actually. A nonstop need to bolt to the door and be loud, reckless, and alive has been biting at my toes for a while, and that doesn't match James's need for the safety of dead quiet.

"Coming here with him wasn't smart," I say. "I thought since New York has so much to do, we'd explore and reconnect, but nothing has changed." Except me, as I've tried to make myself what James needs. "I can get a ticket and fly out this afternoon."

"I'm sorry it didn't work out. Maybe you need time apart. And about Christmas…we're in Quebec, remember?"

What are my parents doing in Canada? It's colder there than in New York.

"Nope, I don't recall Quebec."

"Mom didn't mention it? Huh." There's shuffling and mumbling. "Oh. Mom says she didn't want to bug you with details during your busy season. We figured since you and James couldn't make Christmas, we'd head up north. She's always wanted to see the nativity tour, so we're staying in Old Quebec, and they've decorated everything—I mean everything. We've walked into a Dickens Christmas village."

"That sounds nice. Chilly, but nice." I don't want to go to Canada. It doesn't have my carousel or smell like cinnamon pinecones.

"It is. I'd tell you to come here, but we could only book because someone canceled two minutes before we called. Hang on, and I'll go see if there's another room available."

"I don't want to interrupt. Can I go to the house?"

Dad hisses through his teeth. Ooh, that's going to be a no.

"Oh, well, you know that Airbnb thing?" he asks, and I visualize him scrunching his face and biting his lips until his mouth disappears into his dark, gray-speckled beard. "A family rented the house for the week."

"You let someone rent the house?" I take a long gulp from my cup, washing down the last vestiges of hope for a normal holiday.

"Yeah. They're pleasant folks. Just a family wanting to visit the lake during the winter vacation."

"What if they steal everything?" Someone is sleeping in my

bed right now or staring at the old photos on my pin-board. I don't live there anymore, but it's the house I grew up in, and my parents didn't change my space.

"We locked up the important stuff."

"What if they have six dogs that eat all the furniture? Oh! Or they make a porno on the couch?"

"Cozette," he chides. "Like that couch hasn't seen its fair share of—"

"Dad!"

He laughs in rolling melodic waves. "Sweet pea, it's fine. I'll check on an additional room and call you right back."

We hang up and I pull out my laptop, opening emails. There's one request for location research on the East Coast. Easy peasy. Another requests a forty-person full workshop design in Portland. Fun.

Too bad I didn't have any clients over Christmas; otherwise, I could pop into one of the events I plan. Some of my clients beg me to show up in person to the conferences I set up while sitting on the couch in my yoga pants. Not having to wear a suit and heels is a massive bonus after years of doing so.

I accept the two and get to work creating new client spreadsheets. I may not know where I'll sleep tonight, but these electronic folders are perfect: ordered, to the point, and exactly like the others—on the path to success with little fuss.

I've planned gatherings my entire life, starting with my fourth birthday party. When Dad told me that taking my ten best preschool buds to Disney World's princess castle wasn't within the budget, I sat on his lap and instructed him to look for something similar. We found a princess and unicorn duo that would come to the house for pony rides and pictures. The decorations and details were easy once the entertainment fell into place.

After that, it was friends' parties and school functions, then city festivals. By the time I graduated high school, I'd built a résumé that some people twice my age with full college degrees didn't have yet. A huge, international conference company hired me two weeks out of high school, and each year I received a higher title and more demands of my time.

I just get it, and I love it—the budgets, the people, coordinating a hundred things at once and having parts go wrong. There's a thrill in having to turn on a dime and work a secret miracle to keep things appearing like they're not falling to pieces. Everything about it is what I want in a career, except for the hours. There was no life outside of conferences. I faced hundred-hour workweeks and so many flights, I'll have frequent flyer miles for a decade.

I made so much money in exchange for my early twenties.

My phone beeps.

It's James. *Hey, where did you go? Come back home so we can talk.*

Nope.

The phone chimes again, and this time it's Dad calling.

"Hi," I answer and brace myself for a very wintery holiday.

"Bad news, there's nothing available. The nearest vacancy is miles away, and the innkeeper said she wouldn't put anyone she loved there."

I'm sad but relieved. Alone for the holidays, but not destined for the arctic. "That's okay. I'll think of something."

"Need us to come back? We could go to a B&B."

I love my parents so much. "No. You two kids have fun. I'll let you know what I'm doing in a few."

That puts me on the clock. If I don't have a solid location in the next hour, the dad timer will detonate, and my parents will be on a plane and not living out their Dickens fantasy Christmas.

We hang up, and I jump feetfirst into an internet search. The potential Christmas getaways are endless. Disney? Booked.

Christmas spa excursion at Hershey? Booked. A wine country Christmas in Cali? Not this holiday.

Tropical locations keep popping up in my search. Hanging out with Santa by a palm tree while I drink yuletide cheer out of a coconut? *Yes, please.*

The options are daunting. Hundreds of self-proclaimed paradises vying for my attention with deals that may or may not be a dream come true, and in locations I've never heard of.

Helena. I need Helena.

I scroll through my emails to find the best travel agent ever's contact info. She's assisted with many of my out-of-country event bookings and cuts the best deals.

However, booking three days before Christmas? Maybe she can work a miracle.

"Cozette," she says, in a tone that wraps me in a winter hug. "Happy holiday season."

"You, too. I have a request, and it needs to be speedy quick."

I explain my predicament in less than a minute without taking a breath.

"Oh my. Give me your budget, what you're looking for, and I'll see what I can do. You have to leave today?"

I'd get a hotel room, but that's not plan A. As pissed as I am, if James starts his super sad lament highlighting the good times we've had and poses a convincing argument about how we'll work it out, I'll cave. It's best if I surrender thousands of miles away so I have time to come to my senses and realize this has gone on too long.

"I'd prefer it, yes."

"Woman, that's a tough order. Most flights for the tropics leave JFK in the morning, but...maybe today we'll get lucky." Her sweet voice whips to schoolteacher-fierce. "Give me your needs."

She's in business mode, and I love that about her. Someone is on my team.

"Five grand, max," I say. "But I'd prefer under three, a week stay, tropical weather, alcohol, all-inclusive because bikinis don't have pockets, Christmassy, and fun. Oh, but not a family resort. That's entertainment I'm not ready for. Peaceful ocean sounds, sans screaming."

Clicking and scribbling sound through the line. "Mmkay, I have four places in mind and your credit card on file. Do you trust me?"

"I do," I say with a nod.

"Gonna burn up this card. I'll call you with details."

She hangs up without another word, and I smile into my now-chilled beverage. Still chocolaty.

The scowling woman stands and taps her fingers on my table. "Good for you, hon."

"Thank you." It *is* good for me. I'm bailing out of this coldbox and away from Mr. Boringpants. I'll sing drunken carols with surfer Saint Nick and stick my toes in the sand on Christmas morning instead of snow.

I roll up my puffy sleeves and get cracking on venue research to keep busy. The temptation to browse the net for the tropical places Helena could send me is strong, but then I'll fall in love with an unavailable resort, and anywhere else she finds won't hold a candle to my long-lost paradise.

A half hour later I'm tapping my empty cup, boots propped on my luggage. The phone rings, nearly sending me into the air. I fumble it, then answer.

"Get thee to JFK," Helena announces. "Your flight leaves in one hour and twenty-three minutes for Simona Island."

2

SHIRTLESS CHIVALRY

*N*ote to self: Plan reckless walkouts better.

When I plan conferences with clients, every detail is managed long before the event day, because frantic stress makes idiots out of intelligent people. I angle myself toward the window and open my heavy coat to create enough airflow not to pass out. I, Cozette Fay, planner of flawless events, am headed to a mysterious tropical paradise, alone for Christmas, in a corset.

I tap the airplane emblem on my phone. What will it hold when I'm on the ground and near a cell tower? If there are cell towers close to Simona Island. And what if it's not Christmassy at all? James and I would have cooked on Christmas Eve—my family's bûche de Noël and the Simon family's green bean casserole. He reminded me of that in one of the fourteen text messages he sent while I was playing musical airplanes. I'll miss the beloved cake my family has every year and munching on chestnuts while watching Christmas movies. The ocean at sunset while I sample a plethora of tropical drinks will be a decent substitution.

The posed, professional pictures of Simona Island I found

while trying to distract myself from the cabdriver's Indy 500 dreams are of white sand beaches with huts and models walking through a jungle. Hashtag posts on social media take the lion's share of web presence, with pics of couples or incredible-looking meals. Cliff diving seems to be a thing. And the airport resembles a toolshed at the end of a country driveway.

The plane bursts through clouds, angling between a cutout of trees and bouncing down on the Simona Island runway.

I have arrived.

It's not a toolshed. The Simona Island terminal is the color of pre-puffed dandelions surrounded by deep green ferns and palms. It's the size of a hundred-person conference hall, with tandem sling seating, a few desks, and one unloved stanchion set that I'm sure rarely has to direct a line. There's no gift shop or restaurant or winding luggage mover, but it's flush with a diverse array of smiling people in shorts and green airport staff tees. They hug everyone, even poofy me in my clunky boots.

There are few people, just my flight's passengers, who separate between a baggage claim window and the double-door exit. Now that I'm not in a panic and sprinting for an airplane, the squinty-eyed stares are more noticeable. I'm bundled up like it's thirty degrees, when in reality it's eighty. They probably think I have some hypothermal condition or that I'm smuggling something. The brief relaxation of getting off the plane and to the location that is an actual island flutters away and my shoulders rise.

I stick my pillow under my arm, toting my purse and carry-on toward baggage claim while flipping off the airplane setting on my phone. The first ding is a text, telling me my luggage is still at San Juan. "No," I say, too loud, scattering the people who were already leery of the woman who doesn't know how to dress for the tropics.

"Ma'am, are you okay?" a male voice with a slight accent

asks as I'm going through my phone to see what magic Helena has concocted to get me where I need to be.

I scroll through emails, not lifting my gaze. "No. Not really. Trying to find the place I'm headed to. Blue..." I'm so frazzled, I've forgotten the name of the resort. "Blue, blue—"

"El Escape Azul?"

My gaze pops up to eyes the color of tropical waters. "Huh? I mean, yeah. What?"

He's tan, scruffy, and his hair is a mess of defined waves only made possible by beach days. His smile has two teeth askew enough to be rebels among a row of perfectly poised soldiers.

"You're not headed to El Escape, are you?" he asks.

"That's the name! Yeah, I am." I wince, because even children know not to give out personal information, yet here I am telling a handsome stranger my vacation spot in a foreign country.

He holds his hand out. "I'm Nico. I'm driving the shuttle this morning. You must be one of my five." I like his light accent. He misses half his Rs. It's European of some kind.

"Cozette." I shake with a firmness learned from my conference days and am met with equal tension, making me smile. There's nothing worse than someone with a floppy noodle handshake.

"Fantastic." He glances around, then back at me. His eyes drag over my coat and boots and land on my pillow. "Um, can I get your luggage and are you traveling with another?"

A bead of sweat trickles down the back of my neck, and I think the steel boning of the corset is leaving grill marks on my rib cage. "My bag didn't make the flight." I take an exhausted breath and check my phone again. "And will spend the night in the airport. I, uh, traveled alone."

A lump in my throat has me swallowing hard. I shouldn't have pushed to get out of New York so quickly. If I'd have thought this out better, I could have had backup clothes in my laptop case after packing properly or even grabbed clothes from my checked bag before throwing it on the rolling luggage bye-bye machine. I wouldn't be carrying around a throw pillow and avoiding the gaze of the hot chauffeur who probably only carts couples around in paradise.

"Ah, that's unfortunate." He wrinkles his nose. It's straight and extra adorable scrunched up. "The luggage, not coming alone. Alone is nice. El Escape has a lot of things you'll like—snorkeling is a favorite. Come on, I'll take you to the shuttle and come back for the others."

I step in line with him. "What if I hate water?" If there were an ocean beside me, I'd be in it. I think the corset could pass for swimwear if I were swimming.

"Then you can dance at the club."

"And if I don't dance?" I'm tempted to shimmy, but force myself to stay stoic because I'm curious about the grin he's fighting to hold back.

"Arcade."

A gasp escapes. "You have an arcade?! I mean..." I clear my throat and get back to this serious conversation. "What if I don't play games?"

Mischief twinkles in his eyes as if he's hidden presents somewhere. Yeah, okay, so this is a much-needed game right now.

"Horseback riding?" he asks.

"I might be allergic," I answer rapid-fire.

"Massage." He responds just as quick, tucking his lip under his top teeth when he's not speaking.

I grimace. "Aversion to touching."

His face falls, and he shrugs one shoulder. "There's always beer and rum."

"There we go." I laugh as we step outside, and hot air engulfs my face. I'm sweating in my parka, which is murdering

Holiday Hotel 19

my enjoyment of the surrounding palm trees, red flowers the size of my head, and an unfamiliar but welcoming birdsong.

Nico pauses at a sleek blue van with *El Escape Azul* painted on the side. If he's a kidnapper, he's a dedicated one. The door slides open.

"Can I take your coat?"

Ah, there's the question. I'm frying, and if I pass out from heat exhaustion, they will take it off me anyway.

"I, um...I have had a day. Flew out of New York City and well, just..." I dance my fingers over the pillow. There's no way to explain this without it being an overshare. "I broke up with my boyfriend while wearing a teeny, festive outfit, tossed on a coat, called the travel agent, and after a whirlwind travel itinerary that didn't include time for a backup shirt, I'm here. Do. Not. Laugh."

Please don't laugh. I'm not sure I'd ever recover if I got rejected *and* laughed at over this getup in the same twenty-four hours.

He gives me a quizzical look, crosses his heart, and snaps his fingers like he's made a magical oath where he will age twenty years or get poison ivy in the no-no place if he goes back on his word. Good enough for me.

In a quick move, I set the pillow in the van and shuck my coat, handing it over. Air caresses my heated skin and I fan my face. Holly bells, that feels amazing. He bites his lip, not in that playful way from a moment ago, then brings his eyes up to mine.

I blow out a lengthy breath and continue fanning the delicious tropical air over my exposed, sweaty shoulders. "I've changed my mind. You're welcome to laugh. May as well. This —" I swat at the white feathers lining the teeny skirt that peeks out over the black sweatpants. "Is ridiculous."

"It's not ridiculous." The double doors fly open, and a couple I recognize from the plane freezes at the sight of me. "El

Escape Azul transport?" Nico asks, taking a half-step in front of me as I take a half-step behind him.

The woman points toward a waiting taxi and they move along, chatting rapidly in another language that sounds similar to Spanish.

I grab my pillow again and white-knuckle the fabric as I hold it to me. I'm not a shy person. At the hotel, if it is a hotel, I'll buy a teeny bikini that will provide the tiniest tan lines, but I'll wear it on a beach with everyone else wearing swimwear. A red velvet corset is out of my comfort zone, especially when I'm baring mucho cleavage to a near stranger. At least I'm cooling down. Except for my cheeks.

Nico turns, putting himself between me and the airport doors. "It's Simona Island; people walk around in tiny, interesting things frequently, but would you like a shirt?"

I unclasp my cramped fingers from my square bodyguard to fan my face. I hope I don't run into this guy after this.

He reaches back and tugs the neck of his blue shirt up and over his head, then drops fabric that smells of salt, vanilla, and a hint of coconut over me. *Oh, wow.* His shirt. That was unexpected. He holds the pillow as I thread my arms through the sleeves and tug the tee into place.

"Thank you." I avoid his eyes for fear of finding pity, disapproval, or that look people wear when they watch a train wreck of a person do stupid shit. They want to pull their gaze away because it's uncomfortable and awkward, but they can't because what happens next is an utter mystery they must unravel. I'm not doing anything stupid though. I'm someone stuck on the train, and I'm trying to exit pseudo-gracefully.

My sweatpants and boots are sweltering in the heat of an unknown island I've run off to three days before Christmas. I'm anti-graceful. Eyes burning, I sniffle and study the clouds.

Nico makes a pity-huff and palms my shoulder with a careful touch. His thumb sweeps back and forth, cool compared to my five-hundred-degree coat. "Hey," he says. "Whatever happened in New York is back there. Simona Island is the perfect place to leave everything behind."

The kindness of his words doesn't match the pointed inflection. They're too...serious. Is he speaking from personal experience or as an observer?

He straightens, interrupting my pondering. With a grin, he hands me my pillow and opens the back of the van. "Can I put your bag back here?"

"Thanks." I hand my stuff over and check out the lifeguard body he's sporting as he places my bags in the cargo area. James is a long-distance runner, all lengthy muscles and no fat. But Nico...Nico is thick shoulders, a sculpted torso, and chivalry.

"Oh, wait!" I hike my sweatpants to my knees, step out of my clunky boots, and set them in the van. "May as well own this look, right?"

When I get to where we're going, I'm going to bathe, eat, and drink a lot of alcohol to forget about this day.

"It will be the height of island fashion by morning." He shuts the van door and points around to the front. "How about you make yourself comfortable and I'll go grab the others. You can sit wherever you like."

"Driver's seat it is."

"Fine by me. Though you had a better chance to reach the pedals in those boots."

I head toward the van's open door. "Don't tempt me. I don't get to drive much in New York, and I'm out of practice. Who the heck knows where we'd end up, and then what would your boss say?"

He gives me a wicked smirk over his shoulder as he walks through the airport doors. "He'd laugh."

3
CHRISTMAS PALM TREES

Nico returns to the van with two couples and a gentleman in a tan, nicely cut suit with a smile that is huge and porcelain against his dark skin. Nico shakes the man's hand, standing tall. He's only wearing swim trunks, but his demeanor is pure business. They talk with familiar, friendly murmurs I can't catch. The man leans close and whispers something to Nico, then claps him on the shoulder, unfazed by his bare torso. I guess Nico was right that people here walk around in whatever.

His laughter carries through the open van door when he sees me hanging out in the driver's seat. "Everyone, meet Cozette. She'll drive us to El Escape if she can reach the pedals and memorize the island's road maps in the next three minutes." He raises an eyebrow at me, and the couple closest to me waves.

I grin back. "The go-pedal is the one on the right, correct? Now where are those keys?"

The woman who climbs into the first row of the van reaches out to give me a dainty handshake. She's wearing white capris, a floral shirt, and sunglasses that take up most of her face.

"I'm Linda and not nervous at all about your driving capabilities." She nods assuredly.

"What if I tell you I live in New York City?" I ask, crinkling my nose. "And that I haven't driven in three months?"

"In that case, I'll be nervous for the both of us," answers the man behind her. He's almost bald, but it works for him. "I'm Phil. We're from Minnesota." He settles next to Linda and places an arm around her.

"Nice to meet you both, and sorry about Minnesota. It must be negative ten there." The warm air can't stop my shiver at the thought.

They both give a weary sigh.

"It is," Linda says. "This is a much-needed break." She settles a hand over a puckered scar on Phil's knee, and he kisses her head.

The other couple is young and starry-eyed, but only for each other. They talk in whispers, giggling and touching. Ah, newlyweds.

I reach for a place inside me that's not bitter. James never acted that way with me—all handsy and sweet nothings. These two are adorable, but at the moment I consider whacking both of them with my throw pillow.

James always treated me as if I were fragile and PDAs were off-limits. Maybe it was because he met me at a trying time. I was exhausted and unsure of my future after leaving my job.

Maybe I haven't been myself for longer than my James era.

At first, I liked how careful he was with me, even with flirting—but still, I lost my giggles soon after meeting him. When a behavior isn't rewarded, it disappears. What else did I used to do that I've forgotten about? Did I lose myself when I met James, or did he help bury me deeper when I'd already encountered an avalanche?

The back door slams, and Nico jumps in the passenger side, dangling a key ring at me.

I refrain from swiping at them like a cat after a dangling string. "You cannot be serious," I say, giving him a challenging glare.

He smirks and bobbles his head in time with the swaying keys. *Tease.* I snatch them and fiddle with the thick black rectangle to get the key to pop out, but it's just a rectangle. What the hell?

"Oh no, she's been bested by the new technologies." He wiggles his fingers in the air. "Give up yet?"

"Never." I check for an ignition slot, but there's only wiper and light levers, a dashboard with a dark screen. "Holy ho ho ho, what mischief is this?"

Linda and Phil laugh, and I glance back to see the newlyweds doing their newlywed thing. I should surrender before the van starts rocking.

Nico grins in triumph as I step out of the driver's side.

He meets me at the front and takes the keys. "It has a push button ignition in the console. Hop in and be my navigator."

I try for a mock sneer, but my facial muscles won't listen and instead drag my lips up as I make my way to the passenger's side. "What kind of chauffeur are you, letting strange ladies in weird outfits do whatever they want? You would have let me drive?"

"Pssh. If you could turn on the vehicle? Of course. This is Simona Island. We aim to please." He tucks his lip under his teeth again as he reaches for the door. "Are you pleased?"

My grin is impossible to tame. "Yeah, I am."

Nico calls the hotel to tell them he has everyone in tow and to make a note to pick up my luggage tomorrow. He hangs up, then types away on his phone for a moment before rapping his fingers against the wheel. "We're off."

As we make our way on tiny roads, he points out a couple of landmarks—a suspension bridge between sharp green mountains just visible over the tree line, and an abandoned tower that was a marker for planes before the airport was built. Simona is a fourteen-square-mile private island, owned by a man who purchased it sixty years ago and named it after his beloved wife. They lived here, slowly building the island into a getaway with enough amenities like medical, grocery, and supply stores to support an active, free-spirited lifestyle, but not enough to overtax the natural landscape or become a commercialized hub of overtourism.

Nico mentions the hotel in passing, instead sharing lore about a mythical creature called the Moss Monster that is said to live in the forest next to the cliffs and lure young, delectable lovers to their doom—so don't wander away without a guide. I find myself curled in the seat, engulfed in vanilla and coconut, facing him as he spins an alluring tale of this magical hideaway.

His eyes twinkle and his hand frequently leaves the wheel to point at things we pass or roll along with his words. Mid-sentence about how many species of birds inhabit the area—fifty-six, according to a world-renowned bird-watcher who stayed on the island for a month—he waves out the window. A woman with thick dreads down to her waist rides a chestnut horse along the road. She lifts her wide-brimmed leather hat high in the air in greeting. Even the horse seems to bob its head and flick its tail in happiness.

This is a man who loves his job, and I bet his job loves him too.

We turn at a blue-lit sign, and excitement darts around inside my body at the five-story building tucked among a bed of ferns and flowers. Alcoves of white stucco and bump-outs of blue-tinted glass squares take turns in a checkerboard pattern along the entire building. Substantial balconies with sofa-like chairs lay between each glass section. Past the modern building, a little solar-roofed hut and the ocean peek through palm trees. I lean as if my motion will magically veer the van around the building so I can get a full view of the blue water that matches the color of the windows.

I appreciate surprises. This, however, from the rainbow of flora to the interesting lines of a clearly new building to the adjoining beach on a private island...I'm flabbergasted. Helena is getting a fruit basket.

We've slowed, and I glance over to see Nico eyeing me.

"What do you think?" he asks.

"I think it's going to be a glorious week."

"It will be." He pulls the van under a covered parking area at the front doors. Two men and two women in blue polo shirts and khaki shorts wave from the sidewalk.

Linda makes a pitchy squeal from behind me and claps her hands. "We're here!"

"Welcome to Simona Island," says one of the men as the van door opens.

The others greet us with waves and bright smiles.

Nico comes around to open my door. I step out of the passenger side, grabbing a few bills from my purse to hand to him, but he waves me off. "It's an all-inclusive hotel—no tipping. But thank you."

"Yeah, but—"

He holds a finger up. "Strict company policy. We don't want visitors to worry about anything while they're here. Stressing about who to tip and how much isn't allowed."

"Well, aren't you quite the rule follower?" I grin at him.

"I am," he tells me with enthusiasm and walks me over to the greeters with his palm against the small of my back. "Cozette, this is Ilaria. She's lived on the island for forty years and can tell you everything about everything. I'll be right back." He wanders to introduce the others.

"Nice to meet you, Cozette," Ilaria says with a pretty lilt, taking my hand in both of hers. "I'll be your personal concierge during your trip. If you need anything at all, you will have me on speed dial during your stay."

Concierge? Sneaky Helena *is* Santa Claus.

"Thank you. It's beautiful here. Nico was regaling us with tales of the Moss Monster."

Ilaria shows off a mouthful of small, pearly teeth. "Yes, those myths kept my daughter out of trouble, mostly." She purses her lips in a proud taunt.

Nico returns and hands me my pillow, then passes my bag and coat to Ilaria. "Ilaria will take excellent care of you, and we will bring your luggage tomorrow. I can provide you with a few more shirts if you need them until then." That tucked-lip thing he does is a dead giveaway to his teasing. It pops out, and he glances at Ilaria. "Oh, or Ilaria can show you the gift shop, but it has limited clothing. If you're so inclined, you can schedule a private jet to the mainland, where there's a mall."

"I'll make do. Thank you, Nico." He was a pleasant welcome to this place. Too bad he saw me frazzled and sweaty in a corset and now I have to hide from him for the rest of my stay. Except to return his shirt.

"Enjoy El Escape, Cozette."

"I will," I tell him, matching his serious tone.

He holds my eyes until he gets back into the van and runs a hand over his mouth before gripping the wheel. The youngest of the two men lifts his chin like he's showing off his strawberry blond almost-beard as he makes his way to the passenger's side and waves at us, grinning as the van pulls away. Everyone here is so friendly.

I take a deep breath and face Ilaria, whose dark-brown eyes crinkle at the edges. She tilts her head toward the doors, bouncing her shoulder-length black spirals that glisten with little streaks of silver. "Ready?"

So much. "Sure." I wave at Linda and Phil, then the honeymooners who aren't paying attention. "I'm sure I'll see you all around. Have so much fun."

"You, too, Cozette," Linda says as they head inside.

I ooh and ahh at the whimsical twisting lighting, white surfaces, and pops of orange that tie in a clean, modern design. The seating is sleek but plushy enough to make me want to curl up with a book. A map of Simona Island takes up most of a wall next to a Christmas tree decorated with silver and gold ornaments and shells.

Ilaria waves at the front desk attendants, standing behind a glowing blue egg that's draped with ferns decorated with festive ribbons. The woman with nearly shaved teal hair and a mask of freckles introduces herself as Jennifer and passes me a clipboard to sign while she checks my passport, then Ilaria and I follow the glass floor tiles patterned in a wave. She doesn't appear bothered by my odd attire and points down a hall with a hot pink manicured fingernail. "There's the shop where you can get sunscreen, clothing, bags, and souvenirs. Around the corner are the cafe and dining hall. The spa is downstairs." She directs me to the elevator. "You're from New York City?"

"No. I'm from North Carolina, but I've been living up there for a few months."

"I've never been to the city, but I watch every musical that comes out on video and download every soundtrack I can find."

"I've been to a few shows."

"Really?" Her lips part as if she wants to ask, but she pauses, then smiles. "I've always wanted to go, but I want to take at least a couple of weeks, and finding time like that can be difficult."

Don't I know it. It's hard to get away from events and the tourist industry. Especially if you love what you do, which she seems to from her bubbly bounciness. "On Broadway, everything is good." At least it was when I went on a high school overnight field trip and smashed three shows into our itinerary.

We step up to a brushed nickel elevator, and as soon as

Ilaria pushes the button, it opens. It's fancy inside, with pristine mirrored walls. Ilaria pushes the number five, igniting a soft white glow. She explains the schedule for food—whenever I want something. Drinks—just call for delivery. Activities—the island is my merry little oyster.

I'm tempted to hopscotch the hallway of plush carpet patterned with beige and blue waving lines, but I don't know this person yet. There's a lot of space between each dark wood door, recessed in a lit blue alcove, and I try to figure out the layout of the rooms. There are only five glowing blue spots down the long hallway. Maybe they're shallow? The upper floor wasn't smaller, because the building is a box. At least the front side is, but why would the upper level be so narrow?

She turns to an entry pad on Room 5-C and scans a card that hangs on a lanyard around her neck. The buttons give beepy whispers under her fingers. "Okay, Cozette, type in a four-digit number you can remember so you can get into your suite. You can also use that code to pay for spa experiences and shop items."

"Ah, what a good idea." I enter Dad's birthday month and year.

The door opens and my voice escapes in a squeak. Floor-to-ceiling windows display a hundred shades of blue between the sky and ocean. There's a couch with a wild geometric pattern and plushy bright pillows and blankets, a desk, and a kitchenette of glass cabinets and marble counters. A Christmas tree twinkles in the room's corner. White lights, sapphire and silver balls, and a variety of ocean-themed ornaments like starfish and sand dollars deck the fake balsam pine.

"It's so beautiful," I whimper and step inside. The living room carpet is thick and soft.

Ilaria wasn't kidding—this is an actual suite. I thought I had a standard room, but this is twice the size and doused in luxury. There's an open door I follow to a teal bedroom with a huge lit wreath above a king-sized bed. The comforter is white—acceptable with the bright walls—and has a team of pillows, some white, some orange, cuddling against the bamboo headboard. I add mine to the mix and sure enough, the swirling mandala of colors looks perfectly in place, except mine is missing its mate. I should have taken them both from that dark, cold world of beige.

"This is *not* a standard room," I say, staring out the wall of windows to the balcony. Palm trees dot white sand like candy canes sticking out of snow. Couples sit in lounge chairs or walk hand in hand down the beach. I won't loop my arm in the crook of James's elbow ever again, but it's fine, I think. I need a book, coffee, and that balcony.

"Well, when the boss asks if there's an available suite for an upgrade and there happens to be two, you get my favorite."

"The boss?"

"He's so secretive." She throws me a wide grin like we've been friends a good, long time. "He hates it when I call him that. How long have you known Nicolai?"

Wait, what? I turn as she sets my bag on the dresser and opens a drawer. "Nico? I met him at the airport." He drove the van. Shirtless. Not that there was anything wrong with that. I rather enjoyed the tour and show, but he's so…I rub at the wrinkle between my eyebrows. *Fun.* He was fun and kind and completely disarming. "He's the boss?"

As she hangs my coat in a closet between the room and bathroom, her smile fades. She studies my face and straight-up winces. "Ooh, oh my. I thought with the shirt," she says, signaling to my attire. "And he doesn't make requests such as this one. He didn't explain." Her voice continues to elevate in distress. "And the way he…ai, apologies, Cozette. I thought you two were…friendly."

I crack a smile. "He's very friendly."

"He, uh, is." She doesn't seem comforted by that though.

"He's also very private and does not like anyone to know he's the owner of El Escape."

"Oh." Not just the boss, but the owner. How? What? My thoughts scatter like snowflakes in a gust of wind. I've met a lot of owners of hotels and corporations, and I couldn't picture one of them driving a van shirtless. Even the owner of the van company.

Why does he pose as a driver? Maybe he's tired of sales calls. Or maybe he likes to wear Santa swimwear without judgment. Oh! Or maybe he's a rich Mafia heir hiding from other mobster families. He was gangster charming, after all.

I raise my hands up in a shrug. "Well, I thought he was kind and down-to-earth." And hot as noon in the tropics. Entertaining too. "His secret is safe with me. I won't say anything."

She takes a relieved breath. "Thank you. He'd appreciate that, as would I." She glances around the room, then back at me. "Would you like to dress and then I can take you for a tour?"

"My luggage was delayed and, in my haste, I didn't pack my carry-ons properly. Hence the shirt." I signal to Nico's shirt. Nicolai, the owner. So weird. "I need to stop at the gift shop. Also, I'm starving." I tilt my head to the side and stretch my neck. "I took a flight out at ten-thirty this morning and have had cookies and a pack of peanuts since then."

She shoots me a real grin and pulls out her phone. "Then how about I get some appetizers and drinks sent to the shop? We have bathing suits and they are fabulous."

I give her an appreciative smile. I can forgo a shower for food and alcohol. Besides, what would I dress in? "Sounds perfect. Show me this paradise."

4

TOURIST FAIL

The gift shop fits like a cozy heart inside the hotel. It doesn't have fancy, luxury resort clothing, but unique handmade items at decent prices, an array of trinkets, reading material, and snacks from all over the world.

I raise my arms, dancing to the club music piping through the speaker above the dressing room, and take a last glance in the mirror. The sundress's plunging neckline dips to a silky coral-colored sash around the waist. "How about this one?" I say, shoving aside the curtain to strike a magazine model pose for Ilaria.

Sitting on the big orange ottoman beside her, Nico blinks at me, a cheese fritter in his fingers frozen close to his lips. I'm certain they've increased the shop temperature twenty degrees, and I barricade myself back in the dressing room, fan my face, and laugh-whine. "How have I met you twice and boobed out in front of you both times?" And also misplaced my word filter.

Ilaria's laugh is a sweet ripple of sound.

"I could offer you my shirt again," Nico says, and I can hear the smile in his voice.

"You are going to run out of clothes if we keep meeting like this." I bite my lips together to prevent myself from telling him that would be the best thing to happen all year. Nico shirtless was an early Christmas present.

"I told you before, you're in the right place to—" He laughs, a wide-open reverberation that makes my grin stretch ear to ear. "I can't even say it."

"Boob out?" Ilaria offers. "It's perfect, Cozette. It will work beautifully for dancing tonight."

Ilaria is making it her duty to inoculate me into island vacation mode as quick as possible and has our evening planned. Not mine...*our*. She's forcing me to ride along blind for once, though going with someone else's flow isn't the easiest thing to master in a few hours. I give myself a stare-down in the mirror. *You are officially off the clock of responsibility for those around you, Cozette Fay. Go with the motion of the Caribbean ocean.* "Do we still have drinks?" I ask, putting Nico's shirt back on and opening the curtain.

His legs are spread, arms crossed as he leans against the wall, a slow smile spreading as his eyes wander my—his shirt. His posture is a request. It says, *Straddle me, Cozette.* If I wasn't amid a breakup, I'd answer that call, pseudo-stranger or not. Place a hand on his chest, settle over him, and see how silky his waves are under my fingers.

"Mmm, we're low." Ilaria pops up, holding two drained glasses. "I'll get you another."

"No," Nico says, eyes still on me. He stands and stretches, shirt rising to show off drawstrings and sharp hips. "I'll send something over. I have stuff..." His words trail off and he grins and runs his hand through his hair. "I'm sure we will catch up later. Uh, Ilaria." He poofs out faster than Santa up a chimney.

Ilaria turns her raised eyebrow to me. "You see why there was confusion, right?"

I gasp. "I do not know what you mean," I say with mock confusion, touching my fingertips to my chest, over Nico's shirt.

The subtle El Escape Azul imprint blazes up at me, mocking the obviousness of this moment, and I duck back into the dressing room to try on a shirt that is not Nico's. "Okay, fine. He's fun to look at."

"You're not the only one looking, Ms. Cozette. I wish—"

I scrunch my face and poke my head out. "You wish?"

"Nothing." She stands, giving me a coy grin. "You look ready for an evening adjusting to tropical life. Want anything else?"

Knowing that wish would be nice. Instead, I grab my treasures. "Um, sunscreen for tomorrow, flip-flops unless I want to go in snow boots or stilettos everywhere, and..." I know what people do on vacation, but doing those things seems so foreign. "I think I'll shower and get through this night, then reevaluate." Read? Sit on the beach, probably. I should be making Christmas goodies and doing last-minute decorating, but I have no goodies to make nor things to decorate.

"Hello," a man sings, approaching with a tray holding a coral-colored drink and a small bowl of fruit drizzled with cream sauce. His sculpted mohawk is bleached, and he wears round tortoiseshell glasses above the biggest grin I've ever seen. His eccentric style melds together with a pink flamingo print button-down, sparkly bow tie, and super short shorts. "I heard there was a new beauty needing tropical sustenance stat."

I smile and take the offered drink. "Thank you. This will erase everything up until now, right?"

"Aw, you know my secret recipe," he croons. "I'm Walt, the head bartender here."

"Pleasure to meet you." I sip and my eyes roll back. It's fruity fizz, not too sweet and a little citrusy. "This is the best past-erasing elixir the world has known. I'm Cozette."

"I've heard." He winks and passes the bowl to me. "Enjoy and come dance later. We have an instructor who'd love to get his hands on you." With a spin and a wave like he's a parade princess, he leaves me with deliciously full hands and more questions.

My eyebrows are getting their exercise today with all the shock and confusion. I aim one at Ilaria. "Nico isn't also the dance instructor, is he?"

"No," she says, her voice long and trailing off. Maybe Nico is a terrible dancer. She leads me to the front of the small room and helps unload my arms for checkout. "Though he may join *you* if you ask."

She offers to help me take my new items upstairs, but I'm sure she has better things to do than tourist-sit me, so I head up to my suite, promising to meet her in an hour for a tour.

Showering off airport, dried sweat, and my fight with James is delightful. Doing so tipsy, sipping rum punch, ups the pleasure, and knowing that a beach is four floors and a patio away is the ultimate win. I slip on the new dress, hope gravity behaves if I dance tonight, and make my way to the sliding door, but pause at my laptop. "No," I tell myself. No emails, no spreadsheets, no James. Not today, Santa.

I blow out a long breath and open the balcony door. Salty, warm breeze coasting around a lit kidney-shaped pool, silhouetted umbrellas, and the evening sea sparkling under moonlight clear my thoughts. But the couples holding hands, smooshed together in the dim light provided by strings of Christmas lights wrapped around palm trees, lands me back into my relationship woes, so I back myself into the room again. I go all out on my hair and makeup to keep myself occupied. Fortunately, I took every bit of cosmetics I owned and the flat iron. A knock nearly makes me take out an eye with the mascara wand but I dodge, swipe on a last coat, and stride to the front of the suite to greet Ilaria.

Except it's not Ilaria. Out the peephole is a head of beachy waves, blue eyes, and a lip bite that is not playful. Nico looks nervous.

"Everything okay?" I ask, opening the door and leaning close to him to glance down the hall for Ilaria. No one should smell this good. Coconuts and vanilla should be illegal on men I meet hours after a breakup. I declare it so. He needs the essence of jerky and gym socks. Microwaved halibut in an office with no windows.

"Yes." He crosses his arms, then puts his hands on his hips. Is he...squirming? "Ilaria asked me to give you a tour, and she will catch up soon. She needed to sort through kitchen supplies...apparently."

"Those are quite extensive in resorts." I slip on the new flip-flops and search for a key before remembering the fancy keypad.

"They are." He grins and lets his arms drop. "Is there anything you're specifically interested in seeing, or do you want the standard tour?"

I have walked the depths of every major conference center in the States and more hotels than I can remember. The thought of getting a grand behind-the-scenes glance sends a tremble of nervousness through me. Excitement yes, but anxiety too. I will compare this hotel to others, because as much as the industry hurt me, the physical building where all the nitty-gritty things happen is my playground. I only wish I could let go and be a tourist for once.

"You appear baffled." Nico nods toward the elevator and I follow. "How about we go, and if you'd like to know something, I'll answer what I can."

What he *can*. Mm-hmm. "That would be perfect," I say, biting back twenty questions about hotel services and events, dining capacities and breakout spaces for workshops, if they've hosted corporate seminars with team building activities.

"So what do you do in New York City?" he asks, which has nothing to do with a hotel tour. At my hesitance, he scrunches his face. "Sorry. That was invasive. How about—"

I put a hand up to stop him. "It's okay, you've seen me in a corset. That makes you closer to me than ninety-three percent of all people." My face heats.

The side of his mouth quirks. "Interesting seven percent."

That makes me laugh as we stop at the elevator doors. "Absolutely." I twist my lips for a moment as I think on how to answer. "I haven't been in the city long, so my biggest task has been unpacking boxes and figuring out where stuff lives, but I'm a virtual event planner."

"How does that work?" His head tilts to the side, and his eyes scrunch the slightest bit.

"I pick my clients and my hours, and I work from anywhere I want."

I briefly explain my yoga-pants-and-couch career of spreadsheets and phone calls. Nico is easy to talk to, and I'm tempted to share that the reason I need such a light job is because my previous conference director position made me burn out to a charred shell of a person. But he doesn't need to hear me lament about the last day of my final in-person conference. The final straw that broke me.

Nico leads me out of the elevator, hands in his pockets, but halts in front of a narrow wall table with a huge coral sculpture on it and turns to me. "Why the city?"

"Boyfriend." Wait, that's not right. "Ex-boyfriend, I mean. His company wanted him in Manhattan." It feels like a heavy conversation even for someone in my made-up seven percent. Especially with him so close, his handsome face in an attentive scowl. I want to jam my fingers in the corners of his mouth and drag them upward, but he'd need to be in the upper three for that treatment.

Nico makes a little hum sound I can't define. Like he's asking himself a question instead of me. That is for the better. I don't want to talk about James.

I let out a long breath. "How long have you been here?" I

should have used "worked here" if I'm keeping up with the ruse, and I do an internal ass-kick.

"My first trip was seven years ago." He signals with his head toward the hallway and steps forward. "I'll show you the fitness center and snack kiosk." Since he rolls right into after-hours food services, I take the hint that he doesn't want to talk about his arrival to Simona Island.

We pass a couple of closed doors that have a panel of glass to peek in, but I only get a glimpse as Nico lists dining, bar, and club hours. Multipurpose rooms? For meetings or inside recreation maybe? Did he build this place or buy it from another? Why is there no information online about it?

By the time we're standing in front of the wall map, where he's pointing at landmarks, my mind is in a deep dive of what events they host and Nico's path to hotel ownership, but Ilaria said he likes privacy. His accent is another level of distraction. Is asking where he's from too invasive?

"And I've lost you, haven't I?" he asks, smiling as he points at the Simona Island map. "Cliff diving isn't exciting for you?"

My eyes go wide. "There's cliff diving?" Wincing, I put my hand on his arm. "I'm so sorry. Capacity numbers won't stop rolling in my mind, along with internet bandwidth capabilities and how breakout rooms would work in a boutique hotel. It's a lifelong obsession I can't turn off." I'm failing at vacationing.

When he smiles, I realize he hasn't been doing a lot of that. It brightens his whole demeanor—sun beaming through clouds. He takes my hand and tugs me down the hall before releasing his hold. "Maximum capacity is five hundred, which we'd never have."

"Because that would squish everyone." I've been in maximum capacity situations and work hard to avoid them and help my clients do the same. A room can fit a thousand, if your attendees don't mind cuddling like travelers on a New York subway at rush hour.

"It would," he says with a nod. "And no one likes being that close to strangers...usually." Before I interpret that lip tuck, we turn the corner to the dining hall.

The dim room is two stories tall with a wall of glass overlooking the ocean, and tropical plants throughout the space bring the outdoors inside. Couples feed each other across small, white-clothed tables or stand hip to hip grabbing food from long buffets. Nico explains the catering capabilities, switching to business terms instead of common tour talk. He talks with his hands, spinning fingers through the air as he speaks about the back of the house rollout of courses. He signals to a chandelier that's made of recycled sea glass, and I can tell it was his choice by the pride he wears on his face. His lips raise on the left side, and he leans closer to explain the leftover meal distribution and composting plan, making me want to take notes.

"Sorry." He pauses, wrinkling his nose. "I'm getting carried away."

"Pssh. Carry on. Reducing the environmental impact of large-scale business is important. Did you go to school for that?"

If his eyes are a stage, the curtains just slid shut. "Partially. It was a minor. Did you study event management at university?"

It's my turn to shift uncomfortably. I should be used to the question, but I'm out of practice. I don't see anyone at events anymore, so they can't ask me. My virtual clients couldn't care less about my background as long as I reduce the stress in their lives and make them look like heroes.

Nico clears his throat, raising an eyebrow.

Ah, I should probably speak. He appears as confused about me as I am about him. "No college. I went straight into career-land."

He holds the door for me to the outside patio. "There's nothing wrong with learning in the field."

"I didn't say there was."

"You made a face." He waves at a stunning woman in a lifeguard chair, who grins wide and tilts her head at me.

I wave too, as if we know each other, and she mimics me, confused by the action of her hand. I call that auto-politeness. It's big in the industry. Wave first, identify later. The fall into event mode is so fast, though I should not be doing that here. *Vacation, Cozette. Escape and reset.*

"Did I?" I ask, knowing I made a face. That was an opening question when I was doing live events. Handshake, kudos on the successful event, and then, "What university did you attend?" As well as I did, noticing reactions would either be a joy or a punch to the gut. I shrug. "No matter how many times someone proves themselves, the past still sets some people's perceptions."

I glance at Nico in the marked silence. His brows are furrowed. When he notices my gaze, he nods. "That's...accurate." He puffs his cheeks, blows out a breath, and points. "There's the arcade. It's pretty great in there, but since you don't play games—"

I veer, leaving Nico and his laughter behind me.

He trounces me three times in Skee-Ball, but I annihilate him in air hockey. In the small game room, there's a vintage Whac-a-Mole game, but the third mole gets stuck and makes a clunking sound before the fourth pops up. The fifth doesn't even try to see the light.

"I have bad news," I say, setting the fabric mallet on the machine. "Your moles are unruly."

"It's trauma." Nico holds a serious expression. "Sadly, they've seen too much in their time."

"Oh yeah?"

"Mm-hmm. Are you getting hungry, or would you like me to beat you at racing?" He motions at a seated arcade game with two wheels.

"I'd lap you. Don't change the subject. What did the moles see?"

I move closer and he tucks his lip, shaking his head slowly, eyes twinkling in mischief like he wants me to prod the answer out of him, which I set out to do when my phone buzzes. I rummage through the convenient pockets in the folds of the skimpy dress and wince when I read James's text: *We need to talk.* For a moment I'd forgotten about him, and now he's here, stepping between me and a much-needed flirt session. I should be holed up and mourning my lost relationship—unless it's not lost, and after this impulsive Christmas getaway, I go back to New York and we forge ahead. My face scrunches at the thought. Two years deserves consideration, but my logical side says my relationship expired long ago. I endeavored when I should have escaped.

The play has melted from Nico's features, and he leans arms crossed against the Whac-a-Mole game, staring at the phone in my hand.

I clear my throat. "You have good cell and Wi-Fi service."

"There's a technology person on staff who makes sure everyone who wants it can still access their work and personal accounts." He's flipped back into tour mode.

James's name blinks again along with, *Are you there?*

The surge of joy from playing in an arcade crashes. Oddly enough, as the punctual music from a video game behind me hits its no-lives-left tune. Womp womp, indeed. Avoiding isn't going to make unfinished business easier to navigate but...

No, I respond, then slip my phone back into my pocket. "I would like some rum now."

"We can do that." He pushes off the machine and heads to the door, where Ilaria steps in. "Good timing. Cozette needs rum."

Ilaria holds up a finger and rushes off.

I'd protest and go myself, but this is an alcohol emergency, and I don't know where the nearest bar is.

"What do you need?" Nico asks, with a firm, going-to-fix-it tone. It's an order, but unexpectedly sweet and incredibly comforting. Much like him handing over his shirt like it was no big deal because it put me at ease. If James would have had his eyes on me like this and paid attention to clear shifts in my mood, I might not be alone in paradise.

"Rum?" I answer, mainly in jest. I'm aware that rum does not solve problems, but it does taste delicious.

He raises an eyebrow and waits, as if he understands that I will answer if he's patient enough.

I comb my fingers through my hair as my pocket buzzes again. Twice. "I need time to think, and also not to think. I need more fun than I've had in years, my feet in the sand, and a Christmas unlike any I've ever known." Because the ones I'm used to are not going to happen.

A slight yet victorious grin spreads over his face. "That's more like it."

"Good news." Ilaria pops in with a bright blue drink loaded with fruit. "Peter had a fresh tray. This is called The Escape." She runs her hand through the air with her wispy words and passes over the hurricane glass with a flourish.

"How's the kitchen?" Nico asks Ilaria, pointedly.

"Fully functional," she says with a grin. "Are you two having fun?"

"Yes," I say and moan at the drink. What is it about rum in the tropics?

Another buzz sounds, but it's Nico's phone this time. He drags it from his back pocket, glancing at the screen. His shoulders sink. "Can I trust you two alone for a few minutes? The mole psychologist has to cancel again. I need to make calls to get them the attention they deserve."

I snort into the tart drink and slap a hand over my laughter.

He winks as he slides out the door. "Maybe Ili will share their story if you blink those eyes at her." Turning to her, his expression hardens to commanding determination. There's the businessman. It's only a glimpse, but it's present. "She needs sand therapy. And maybe..." He glances at me. "A walk through the gardens and then the club."

5

PEANUT BUTTER IN A PHIL AND LINDA SANDWICH

I press my eyes tightly closed at the brightness. What time is it, and why does it feel like a Santa Claus-sized man is sitting on my head? I moan and turn my face into pillowy darkness.

The softness under me dips, sending me on an ocean of waves I'm positive don't actually exist. Otherwise, there'd be birds and beach scent, but there's only vanilla and a hint of coconut. I thought I took Nico's shirt off long ago.

Yesterday happened, I think. There was a journey and shopping with Ilaria. Drinking and incredible food. Nico's distracting presence. That makes me smile, though the motion hurts my face. I snuggle back into the pillow and attempt to ignore the invisible tilt-a-whirl I'm riding on. Rum is good here. Like top-notch stocking candy that you eat first, in excess, because you can't help it and are celebrating. I celebrated last night. Toasted to long-missed travel, new experiences, the end of Christmases as I've known them, and a new era of me. I recall a tour of the pool, with its cute little cabanas, and a beach, where I stuck my toes in flawless sand and literally felt the stress shimmy out of my bones and out of my feet. The sand ate it like a happy Labrador, all open-mouthed and inhaling without considering what painful emotions taste like. Ilaria and I sang musical scores and carols together as we took the outside walkways to different areas of the hotel. Then things went rum-fuzzed.

I drift, then wake as the world around me floats off on another journey of waves.

It's quiet here. Quiet and coupley. Everyone is experiencing this paradise with another person. All but me. Oh, and the Whac-a-Moles. Bless their little, plasticky hearts. I snort a laugh into the pillow. With barely a prod, Ilaria gave me gossip on the lifeguard and her tryst with two of the arcade attendants back in the summer. Every year there is an island staff-only event called the Moss Monster Meet, and there is some type of spectacle the residents of the island get to gossip about. This year, the Canadian lifeguard missed the midnight beach run and any chance of becoming champion because the three of them were exploring new ways to use the Skee-Ball lanes, a racing motorcycle, and the poor vintage Whac-a-Mole game that will never be the same.

Turns out Ilaria is a terrible secret-keeper. It's nice to feel more inside with the staff than out with the guests. It reminds me of when I did overnight events. It's amazing how quickly you can become a team and get to know others in the right situations. Besides the throbbing headache, this feels like the right situation.

It also turns out that once Ilaria spills a secret, she needs to wash it down with more things she probably shouldn't share with guests. After she joined me in the rum antics—my stomach does a slow roll of remembrance, making me swallow hard—she shared that she didn't only work at the resort for half of a century, she and her husband sold the tattered building and beach to Nico after a hurricane wrecked it, giving Ilaria an excuse to back away, something she'd wanted to do since Xiamara was little and went through chemo for childhood leukemia. When she spoke of Nico—his arrival and how they worked so well together from minute one—her words were light, but her tone was laced with something unreadable. Something downtrodden. A three on a one-to-ten scale of sad-to-happy emotions. The only thing I could subtly drag out of her was that she wished he could meet someone like me. She said it twice in a wistful tone.

To make up for awkward emotions, I spilled an emetic rendition of my past two years to her in a much-needed therapy session of strangers turned not-possible-to-be-strangers-ever-again. Because of rum and because I needed it. James isn't a fan of my enjoyment of alcohol. He says I get loud and weird. On this occasion, he may have been right. Other dodgy memories flash with neon blue lights, raised glasses, wild movement over a bright Tetris board of colors, and eyes as breathtaking as the surrounding ocean. There was a hallway stagger and laughter. What was I laughing at?

Water pours into a glass, making me startle.

I drag my face out of high-thread-count cotton and squint in the morning light. "Owie," I say, trying to decipher shapes in the moving room.

"What, no elves' bells or Comet's furry ass?"

That makes my reluctant vision clear.

Nico sits beside me in my hotel room bed, under the covers but wearing a shirt. He passes over a short glass of water. "Drink this."

Uh, what happened last night? I'd ask, but my tongue sticks to the roof of my mouth. So thirsty. I chug the water, making impatient hums between each gulp. He takes the empty glass, and I flop back to the pillows and watch the ceiling spin until I can't anymore and close my eyes. The flavor in my mouth is old and tangy, intensified with the churning water in my stomach. I swallow hard. Nope. You're going to stay inside today, hydration. I clearly need you.

"Are you going to throw up again?" Nico asks with I'm-familiar-with-your-pukey-ways nonchalance.

Comet's furry ass. I flip my arm over my eyes and swallow hard. "I barfed?"

"Oh, yes."

"Publicly?" I cringe. *Please don't have destroyed the hotel with recycled rum punch.*

"No. You're a very considerate sick person."

More water pours into an empty glass.

I peek at him from under my elbow. "And you were here through that?" Hotel staff sees so much. I wonder if they have a guest log of bad deeds they talk about through the year. Come July, they'll all reminisce about Nico having a sleepover with the drunken, single Christmas elf.

"You don't remember?" He rubs my shoulder with a knuckle, and I sit up on my elbows, squinting at the light.

"Not entirely." I take the half-full glass from him and look down. I'm in his shirt again. "Did we get busy?"

He grins. "Beyond the barfcapades? No."

Sugarplums, he saw me throw up. That's bad form even for me. "Um, were we going to?"

"No." He raises an eyebrow. "Though your brand of flirting is unequaled."

Oh no. I scrunch my face and take a sip from the glass before lying back again. "Are you going to tell me what happened or make me guess?"

He bites that lip of his, and even though it sends a stab behind my eyes, I grin.

"That could be fun," he says. "Like blackout twenty questions."

My stomach is sore as it squeezes with amusement, and I scrunch my face at the pounding headache settling in my brain.

He takes my glass, refills it from a glass pitcher, and slides from the bed. He tugs his rumpled shirt over a pair of linen pants, walks into the other room, then returns with an ibuprofen bottle. He drops two pills into my palm. "What's the last thing you remember?"

"Laughing hysterically at something and walking down the hall, but everything beyond Walt is fuzzy. Oh, wait! Walt!"

The bartender was so funny. The dancer he'd mentioned when we were in the gift shop was his boyfriend, Jose, an instructor during the day and the party starter who jumps in the crowd to get people up and on their feet at night. Walt does absurd dancing impressions of his guy—arms flailing, legs going directions that don't seem possible for the human body. My head spun between watching Jose dart perfectly around the dance floor and Walt's parody of his love's moves.

"Oh, yes," Nico says. "You made many friends last night."

"I did?"

"Mm-hmm. I thought Phil and Linda were going to steal you back to their room, but you were turning green by that point." He slides back into bed, lying on his stomach, and hugs a pillow. "And we were laughing at nicknames for coconuts as we hop-scotched down the hall under your insistence. You decided everyone should drink out of a hairy bowling ball at least once."

I'm incredibly sad to be missing that memory. "Coconuts do look like hairy bowling balls."

"We decided that term was better than massive testicle fruit."

A ridiculous stream of giggle rolls out of my mouth, and I bite my lips closed. Oh hey, that hasn't happened for a while. Nico smiles widely, crinkling the edges of his tired eyes and catching me off guard with how handsome he is as he lays in the bed beside me. The owner of the hotel.

That's still sinking in. Why wouldn't he want people to

know? Most business owners I've met walk around like rare birds displaying their rich plumage of success. Or they silently scrutinize, wearing an expression that threatens to rip the balls off anyone who would dare to step on the first rung of their triumph ladder. I've only come across a handful who were as ordinary as myself. What about Nico is bad enough to keep who he is on the down-low? What does he do here besides drive the van and give women the shirt off his back? Does he put Christmas trees in rooms, act as a silent partner with a checkbook, or only take care of drunk guests? Maybe he's a rich playboy who bought a hotel to bed vulnerable women. Oh, did we talk about it last night and I don't remember?

Fa la la you, rum punch.

I lick my chapped lips. "I was flirting with you?"

Duh. I don't even know why I asked. He's hot and funny. If I'd had one drink and he was anywhere near me, I was bound to come on to him, even in breakup mode. Especially in breakup mode, apparently.

His face scrunches. "I think so? You told me I could dangle my keys at you anytime and that I had legs. Oh, and that vanilla and coconuts were 'eatable,' which is how we got on the conversation of coconut names. You smile a lot." He smiles too, but it quickly turns around, and he stares out at the early morning sun twinkling against the choppy ocean. "James is a doof. I took your phone away after the third phone call. Sorry."

Groaning, I turn my face into the pillow, flipping back to my stomach. Did I call James, or did he call me? Did we talk, or did I talk at him? He probably gave me a lecture about being too drunk and too loud, scolded me for running away from New York, and ended it with how disappointed he was in my behavior. That or he tried to guilt me because he'd get questioned if I'm not at the party and what will he tell everyone? He can tell them he's a *doof*.

The bed shifts, and Nico splays his warm hand on my back

but stays quiet. Why is he being so nice to a post-drunk, weird stranger? Must be those playboy intentions. Whatever it is, it's working.

I turn my head to look at him. "Why did you stay?"

Most would hightail it at the first heave. The way my body aches, there were many, many heaves. I had a stomach bug once while I was with James. He cracked open the bathroom door, delivered two cans of ginger ale, a pack of saltines, and a tub of disinfectant wipes, then went to his mom's house.

Nico's lips purse, and his fingers rub tingles against my spine. "Because I wish someone would have stayed when I did this." His voice is low, nearly a whisper. "Someone should have taken my phone away."

His pained eyes and frown have me reaching for him, curling against him before I can consider any different reaction. I probably smell, but he doesn't hesitate, turning to wrap his arms around me. He's warm and hard-muscled, thick compared to James, even with his additional inches of height.

I trace his shoulder blade with the hand not pinned between us. "Want to talk about your ex?"

Maybe he already did. He probably explained every question I have about his mysterious self in one momentous night of info-sharing, and I missed it.

"No," he whispers, breath jostling my hair. "But thank you."

I nod. Exes are a hard business. It's odd to be in another man's arms, but this is Nico and for some reason that makes it—

My fingers stop tracing. I have an ex. James and I are done.

I'm free to do as I please. Get drunk and dance for myself, laugh as obnoxiously as I please, and have sex again. With other people.

"Be my rebound guy," I whisper to Nico's mounding pectorals. "I mean...after a shower and once the room stops spinning."

I trace my nose up his chest. He smells even better up close and warm. His neck needs kisses, but my mouth feels like dry skunk. *Wait.* Did I just ask this man to be my rebound guy? Is alcohol still swimming around my brain?

His chest jerks with laughter, but he strokes my hair like this cuddle is a normal occurrence. "I'm not going to be your rebound guy."

"Aw," I whine, eyes closing at his touch. "But we'd have great sex." We must have gotten along great last night if my mind is this comfortable spewing out non-filtered conversation.

He sighs and rolls to his back but keeps me in the nook of his arm. "I have no doubt about that. No fraternizing with guests."

"Pssh. Rule follower. We're snuggling. That's not fraternizing?"

"Good point," he says, a sexy octave lower.

I glance up, and he's biting his lip again. I shove at his chest. "You're a tease."

He laughs and I'm glad for it. It would be uncomfortable if he were to get serious on me, unless he was seriously kissing me. It's not serious though. I may be comfortable with him, but that doesn't mean he feels the same way and this is a vacation. A fleeting, temporary escape. Sure, he's a touchy guy, but not with sharing personal info. Unless he spoke up last night. I recall more, but only his eyes on me and me chattering away, to him, others, and on the phone.

I clench my teeth. Maybe we only talked coconuts before barfageddon. "Did I do anything incredibly stupid I need to worry about?"

He shakes his head, but it's not convincing.

I lift and wince, then reach over him for the other half of the water and take a sip. "Okay, spill it. What did I do?"

He bites his lips together, then lets them pop open again.

"Um, you were the peanut butter in a Phil and Linda sandwich. Just dancing though. You all were having fun."

I wince harder, set the glass down, and press my forehead against his shoulder. "Whoops."

He chuckles. "It wasn't bad. Adorable, actually. I'm not sure if they wanted to adopt you or get it on, but they're in the Cozette fan club."

"At least someone is."

He runs his knuckles down my arm. "I'm a fan too. You're a joy, even when you're rebounding."

I take a deep breath, sit up, and slip from the bed before I kiss-attack him and ruin any chance of future snuggles with my breath. How am I so comfortable with this man? If I would have woken up next to anyone else, I would have screamed or kung-fued their face, but he's so easy to be around. I really am rebounding. I step on cloth and look down to see my pants piled on the floor. Oh, and I'm in underwear. I twist to see blue cotton briefs peeking out from under Nico's disheveled shirt. They have El Escape written over the ass in orange script.

Nico may be a good guy, but he's also the boss and can break whatever rules he wants. Plus, his eyes are taking a slow meander over me, and that blue is looking awfully fiery. He holds his hands up. "For the record, you dressed yourself while I was in the kitchen."

I tug down the shirt and pad toward the bathroom. "Too bad about that fraternization thing. Guess I'll have to rebound myself." I give him an eyebrow flick before stepping into the bathroom.

His groan makes me laugh, but then I catch myself in the mirror and gasp.

Mascara is everywhere and I'm pale. My hair is as unruly as tinsel but not as enchanting.

"Elves' bells, no wonder you don't want to bang me. I'm a drunk raccoon." I pop my head around the corner.

Nico sits up, setting a thick arm on one knee. "You make a pretty raccoon."

My insides would melt if they weren't rum-pickled. "I've got to take care of this disaster, and it will take a while. Breakfast still happening?"

Should we go together or what? Now that I'm farther away from him and have seen my face, the awkward settles in. Where do we go from here? I don't know how to do this. He saw me barf and stayed. That marries people in some cultures.

"It's early still, and you were *ses i hegnet* last night."

"I was...huh?" What language is that?

He stands and stretches, silhouetted against the sunny day. I can't catch his expression with his face shadowed from the surrounding brightness. "Drank a bit. You recover quick, but drink water, eat fruit, and rest on the beach today. Maybe tomorrow you'll be up for snorkeling."

Snorkeling sounds amazing. Actually, it sounds barf-inducing, but I bet later, when I'm hydrated and empty of stale alcohol, it will be glorious. "You going to take me?"

He tilts his head. "Do you want me to take you?"

Oh, Nico. You're so cute. "Do you seriously need me to answer that?"

I should tuck my tail and slink away because this man is front and center for my low point, but he keeps returning for more, and I can't seem to hide from him. All I need now is to have a bawling breakdown and snot all over him. Oh, I hope I didn't do that last night.

He snorts a laugh. "Since you're VIP, we're at your beck and call. I'll take you to my favorite spot."

"I'd like that." I'm probably some karmic challenge for him to tolerate. What did he do to deserve me? I cross my arms and lean against the bathroom doorframe. "VIP, huh? How did that happen?"

Will he fess up and tell me what I already know?

"When there are available suites, the hotel will upgrade incoming guests. It looks good for the hotel and raises ratings." He fiddles with the edge of the comforter, tugging it toward the pillows. "You lucked out. Are you going to leave us a five-star review?"

Lucked out, my ass. "I'll have to see how snorkeling goes."

He grins. "Five stars it is. Have a beautiful day, Cozi." He steps from the bedroom and panic surges through me. What if all this sinks in and he realizes I'm too much? Too weird? He called me Cozi. What did we talk about last night?

"Hey, Nico?" *Just let him go.* I've embarrassed myself enough.

He peeks back around the corner.

"Thank you," I say, weak and trembling. "For being there for me."

"Anytime. Your phone is on the kitchen counter."

The door opens, then shuts with a click. Alone again. The hangover washes off with lime-scented body wash and the cascading bathroom waterfall, and I only nearly throw up once. After a quick brush through wet locks, I head downstairs for fruit. While I'm chowing on melon, I pull out my phone. Oh my Kris Kringle, that's a lot of text messages. I scan to the last one I remember, then read from there.

James: *You were so sweet when I met you.*

I still am, I responded. *But I'm moving on, and if that doesn't make me sweet to you, then that's okay.* Good job me with the logic check even in blackout mode. I even spelled everything correctly.

Other messages are not nearly as brilliant in the rational department, and they're drunker, insultier, and autocorrect clearly gave up all hope.

When are you coming home? he asks.

Nevah evah evah*!@ eeeevvvaahhhhh

We go back and forth, with him finding out I'm flying back to New York on Friday. He told me to get on tomorrow's flight home, that he's paying for my ticket. I sent crying-laugh emojis to him. Then he tells me he's calling. Sure enough, there's a call one minute later in the log. I don't remember it, but it's short.

I pause at one of the last messages from him last night. *I can work on our problems.*

We've played this game often. Give and take, some call it. How often does a couple have to perform this dance to keep walking the same path? How many sacrifices will they make, and how much irritation will they stomach before they explode or their internal self withers away? He would try, and we'd find a new norm of eggshell walking and fitting ourselves into misshapen boxes.

I recall more of the evening, but mainly emotions of rage, inadequacy, and confusion. Snippets of our phone conversations come to mind. James told me he loved me and that he didn't know why I was doing this to him. For a brief moment, in a low point of inadequacy, I didn't either. Why couldn't I make this work? But then he told me he wanted to see me face-to-face to have this conversation, not with thousands of miles and too many rum punches between us. I don't recall his exact words but that was the gist, and it pissed me off.

He only sees me when I'm walking away.

James is a reaction man, and I need someone who lives in the moment with me. Or maybe I need to live in the moment with myself.

Nico's blue eyes locked on mine across the bar table as James told me he had my Christmas present. I told him his was in the closet and what it was—boring running clothes and a gift certificate to the shoe store. I also got him a stress-relief squeeze toy for work. It's shaped like a boob with a nipple and everything.

Nico put one hand over his mouth and the other splayed over the firm abs I knew were under that shirt. It wasn't fair to James for Nico to be right there, tangible and amused.

James scoffed. He'll never even take that boob out of its packaging. He won't even unwrap it knowing what it is, and that's when I remembered why I'm in warm paradise and he's in cold New York.

Then, Linda asked me to dance, and I hung up on him. I hope I'm like Linda and Phil when I'm twice my age. They understand each other—their moves, when they need a break, when it's too much, or not enough. They're two planets in the same beautiful orbit.

Another rum punch courtesy of Walt doing a boneless gummy bear dance, and my thoughts went to events. I may have told Nico, Walt, Linda, and Phil my life story.

The next call, James raised his voice and told me to grow up. Yelled more than told. I spit back that his grandmother was leagues more fun than he was, then let him know the only boob of mine he would ever squeeze again was that stress ball, so he better rip off the paper and get fondling if he was so keen on needing me there.

It didn't make perfect sense, but I was drunk, and Linda was nodding in encouragement at me.

That's when my phone disappeared from the table. Nico brought me coconut water, made me drink it, and when Linda and Phil dashed off for another round with Jose, he asked why I left New York in such a hurry.

My answer was because I needed to be far away when I changed my mind about James. At least I think it was. I tried to explain that breaking up is hard, two years is an investment, I live there and haven't even explored the city yet, but my speech veered to the wayside and dragged my focus with it.

Fucking flurries. That's way worse than looking like a drunk raccoon.

I back out of my phone calls and notice the new contact. In his picture, Nico's eyes are crossed, and he's scrunching his face. His number is right there, tagged *Nico*.

It's hard to finish my fruit with how wide I'm smiling.

Resting in the sun will help me brainstorm a way to thank my helpful business owner friend.

My phone buzzes. My smile drops at James's name. *I want you to come home. Please let me get you a ticket. You can fly out and make it home by this evening. We will cook tomorrow or go to your parents if you want.*

The slight nausea returns, and I sip juice to help steady my stomach. I text back, my irritation itching up my spine and clenching my jaw. *So we can make it to your Christmas party?*

His response is immediate. *I don't care about the party, I just want you home. It's Christmas. I'm sorry about last night. I love you. Call me, please.*

The last part stands out as much as a yellow snowman. I've never seen that in writing from him before.

I chew my lip and tap the table, then stand and dial as I head up to my room.

6

LET'S DO THIS, BEACH

*S*uite life is great. When you text your concierge a request for an ice cream sundae because you broke up for real with your ex, she sends a scoop of vanilla doused in hot chocolate sauce with every imaginable decadence they had in the kitchen, then tops it with a cherry truffle.

I take another bite as I sit on the floor and focus on the tastegasm, which is far better than the numbness from my final conversation with James. I'll still need to go to New York and pick up my remaining things, but then I'm headed to new and exciting adventures. Even if my new, adventurous life starts with rearranging Christmas decorations and lying on the beach like a hungover lump.

Leaning back against the wall of glass in the living room, I toy with a ceramic starfish on the tree. During our phone call, I rearranged the ornaments, exchanging their positions for more impact until they hung in organized lines that draped like a stack of beauty pageant sashes. The silver balls drape below the shells, and the blue ones hang below those. Prettiest tree in all Simona Island.

The beauty of it helps my relief, though I'm still sore—

hungover in two ways. James and I shared a life for a while. There were good things about us that hurt to release. Like our routine and that we like each other, according to James. Those were definitely James-like romance arguments.

But then he told me he could provide for me and we could get married, and I had to tell him firmly that there was no hope for getting back together. The thought blazed stronger than expected. I'm truly done.

And now that my ice cream therapy session is over, there's a beach out there that needs exploring.

Ilaria wasn't kidding about the fantastic array of bathing suits. The gift shop has all kinds. Unfortunately, none of them are Christmassy, but I found a shimmery coal-black one. Close enough.

I don my new, sheer cover-up over the bikini, sunscreen, and flip-flops, then head to the front office to ask when my luggage will be here. The shuttle is on its way. I make arrangements for them to take it up to my room so there's no need for me to leave my lounge chair.

The tile on the back patio matches the color of the white sand. Stairs lead down to the beach, which is cooler under my feet than I expect when I kick off my flip-flops. Rolled towels stick out of a square valet poking out of the sand. I snag one and head toward choppy water.

The day is all blue skies and lots of puffy white clouds that breeze by, randomly shading people on the loungers lining the encroaching wave line. It's hot, but not stifling. Not thick with moisture like it gets on the East Coast. I appreciate that, as my head and heart are heavy enough from the day I've had. The breeze coming off the ocean begins to blow away my morning, bringing the scent of salt.

It reminds me of Nico.

What's he up to after spending the evening with my drunk ass? Probably hiding out until I leave. Though he said he'd take me snorkeling tomorrow. If he decides to put up with me, will it only be us or a group from the hotel?

The sands are well-groomed—clean and rock-free. To the left, far off in the distance, is another island, poking out of the water like a breaching green whale, but to the right the teal-tinted ocean stretches to meet the sky. It reminds me of life and endless wonder.

A man in a polo and khaki shorts trots up to me with a silver tray tucked under his arm. "Greetings. It's a lovely day for a rum punch."

My stomach rolls with the thought and I grimace. "Oh, no thank you. I drank enough rum punch last night to last for the rest of the year."

He gives a tight-lipped grin. "Then more next week maybe."

"Ha!" I cover my stomach with one hand. "Sure, but not today, and I'll be gone by then. How about juice?"

"Make it with pineapple and coconut water, Peter." Ilaria waves from a nearby lounger. Her bikini is traffic cone orange and pops against her skin tone.

"You and that color are style soulmates," I say, then turn back to Peter. "What she said, and thank you."

"Come join us, sweet talker," Ilaria says, waving me over. "We may not have weather like this for a few. Let's enjoy it."

A woman sits beside her under an umbrella. Dirty blonde curls with white streaks peek out from her huge sunhat, and she wears the brightest shade of fuchsia lipstick I've ever seen.

"This is Ruth, the hotel's wedding planner. Ruth, this is Cozette, the conference manager from New York."

Ruth smiles wide at me. "Ili told me about you, dear. Please, join us. When you're old like me, you surround yourself with as many beautiful young people as you can." Her hard accent comes straight from her throat and her "with" comes out like "whiz."

Ilaria has a boisterous laugh, and I grin as it loosens some exploring memories from yesterday. "You run circles around me," she says.

"I like busy," Ruth says. "It keeps my mind off creaky bones and death."

Well, that's one way to put it. She's older, but she can't be more than her late fifties. Her skin is pale, with age spots surrounding her blue eyes. The color is similar to Nico's but lighter.

"I like busy too," I say and take the lounger next to Ilaria. "Well, I used to. Now I pick my schedule."

Ruth chuckles a raspy laugh, making me question her age and smoking habits. "If I picked my schedule, I'd work the exact same amount. Did you burn out?" There's a squint of empathy, as if she understands exactly what I went through.

I nod. "Uh, yes. Very much so."

"But you stayed in the industry?"

"I did. I love it too much to stay away."

That makes her grin. "So what happened?" She turns in her chair, propping her chin in her palm. "If you don't mind sharing. We've all had a...defining moment of clarity at life shifts. Did you?"

"Shifts. I like that." I nod enthusiastically. "Oh, I've never had a clearer life-defining moment." I blow out a long breath and drop my head back to the lounger. "My last conference was a four-day monstrosity with thirty thousand attendees that had me on my feet for nineteen hours each day."

She frowns. "Those are monstrous. Takes a toll on the body and the mind."

"Does it ever. When I got back to my hotel room, I collapsed. A couple hours later, I woke up on the floor and crawled to the bed." I rub my temples at the memory of gut-wrenching stress sobs. "After an eleven-hour exhaustion coma, I fled to my parents' house, sent my army of assistants to finish out open events, and found a job with a remote event planning employer. Now I only take the amount of work I can handle." I shrug at their sad faces. "I love the industry, but it's a needy beast that was consuming me."

"You were brave to leave," Ilaria says. "Some wouldn't."

Ruth gives a hum of agreement.

"I was lucky I'd made and saved enough money to cushion a quick exit and temporary break from the industry. If I had kids or a mortgage? Oof." I shake my head at the thought. "Anyway, weddings? How's that?"

She throws her arms up to hook over the back of her chair and grins, looking out at the blue sea. "Oh, it's a delight. Like watching the end of a romance novel. Mostly. Sometimes you get the occasional spat or ill-guided bride or groom, but things either work out or they don't, and the very next week we start again. Do you plan weddings too?" She raises a pale eyebrow.

"No. I've done festivals, parties, and corporate events from fifteen to forty-thousand attendees, but no weddings. There's too much pressure to make things perfect. Not that there isn't with other events, but getting married is a once-in-a-lifetime, must-get-right moment. Well, hopefully once-in-a-lifetime."

Ruth nods. "That is true. Fortunately, here things tend to be on a smaller scale. Sometimes the couple elopes, sometimes they bring the immediate family, but there's rarely a large event. Mainly under twenty. Nice and personal. No wedding of your own yet?"

I stick my lips out and shake my head. "No. Though my ex asked me today." Waves crash and retreat in a calming cadence.

"He did?" Ilaria asks, her fingers touching below her collarbone.

I wince. I shouldn't have said that. When I settle down somewhere, I'll get a dog to spill all my secrets to. It can bark my words to whomever it wants and people will be none the wiser.

"Sorta. I just got off the phone with him, after finalizing this breakup thing. He said we could get married. His exact words."

"Ai. I should have sent more than ice cream to you," Ilaria says. "I would have come up if I knew. What did you say?"

I crinkle my nose. "I laughed because I thought it was a joke. But he was serious, so I told him we were over for good. Finito...end scene for real." I trail off and fidget with the silky hem of my cover-up.

"Ooh," Ruth says with a sucked-lemon face. "How long were you together?"

"Two years. Broke up yesterday for the..." I tip my head back and forth, dislodging memories. "Third and final time. I freaked out and came here."

A picture-perfect Asian couple splash each other in the choppy waves, laughing open-mouthed with abandon that looks good on them. Why are there so few photos online of moments like that? Probably because it would bring a tidal wave of lovers from all over the world.

She clucks her tongue. "*Here* is a grand place to run to. I did the same."

"Oh yeah?" I could go for some commiseration in this land of loving coupledom.

Her bright lips quirk. "I married the love of my life when I was seventeen. He died twenty years and one day later. I traveled to cope and found myself here, knees in the sand, watching the most beautiful couple recite vows that reminded me so much of Henry's and mine."

"We were just speaking like we always do," Ilaria says, with a smile that's not meant for us.

"It was *your* wedding?" I ask, wide-eyed and ready to "aw" myself silly.

She nods and I "aw" away, then give Ruth a sad glance. "I'm sorry for your loss."

Ruth bats my words out of the air with her hand. "That was nearly thirty years ago, dear."

Flaming chestnuts, there's no way this woman is nearly seventy.

"It still hurts, yes, but I'd do it over again in a heartbeat. That man was everything." She sighs. "Anyway, they invited me to the reception, and I decided on the spot that this place needed me, so I stayed."

"We're so happy you did," Ilaria says, reaching over to squeeze her friend's hand.

They're so sweet. Completely at ease with each other, and my heart flops about in my chest. The friends I had in high school all went to college while I worked. I don't regret it, mostly. The college experience would have been fun, proven by the photos of parties, new relationships, and trips I was invited to only as a voyeur because I was working. People I could consider more than acquaintances would be appreciated, especially now. I've had a few associates in the industry that I bounced ideas off of and passed clients to that didn't fit, but they're still treading in the chaos of conferences, and I've drifted yet again to another ocean. It's not like I see them at Christmas or could call them to discuss my breakup escape.

"Ili only loves me because of karaoke hour," Ruth says and flicks her light eyebrows at me. "I'm a stage diva."

"I'd like to see that," I say. "I'm more of a tavern wench."

Ilaria points at me. "Cozette and I made our own karaoke hour yesterday, except it was mainly Christmas tunes while touring the property."

"Oh, I love this time of year," Ruth says. "We should take over the lounge for caroling."

I grin and close my eyes, taking in the sun's warmth. "You should carol the halls. Know any good baritones?"

"Now that's a fun idea," Ilaria says. "We've never done that before."

"Really? Seems natural if you put decorations in the rooms, and out here." I wave at the nearby palm trees with rope lights winding up their trunks. "And you all live here, right? One big happy family celebrating together."

Ilaria nods. "Yes. Working, but we do all get together around that."

I grin, thinking about the staff celebrations we used to piggyback onto a conference. I'd have the caterer make an additional cake, upgrade hotel rooms to suites, or slip favorite songs and birthday wishes to lounge bands. We were a family sometimes, but for a span of days, not living on an island. That would change the dynamic, though probably for good.

"Ladies." The beach waiter returns and hands me a hurricane glass of coral-colored drink with a kebab of fruit sticking out of it.

"Thank you."

He nods and passes a similar drink to Ilaria. While they catch up on supply checks and whatnot, I pull my phone out to take a quick drinking-juice-in-the-tropics selfie to post to my long-ignored social media pages so my old friends can be the voyeurs for once, then decide against it. That would be weird after so much time. I go to text it to my parents instead, but divert my finger at the last second and choose Nico.

The beach was a good idea, I text along with the photo, then turn back to the women.

Ruth watches me with a friendly yet curious grin until Peter passes her a Bloody Mary with a kebab of shrimp and lemons.

Ruth grins. "Ah, thank you, Peter."

"Anything for you, Miss Ruth."

She bats her hand at him and giggles. "You flatterer."

I give Ilaria a questioning eyebrow raise, and she purses her lips and winks at me. I don't know what that means yet, but I really want to.

My phone buzzes. Nico. *The beach is always a good idea. Feeling better?*

Grinning, I reply. *Much. I didn't realize drinking fruit and soaking in sunshine was the best hangover remedy. If I would have only known, I'd have been here long ago.*

Wait until snorkeling. Tomorrow morning.

Peter wanders off to another couple on the beach, and the stares of the ladies make me put my phone away.

"That looked like a happy message," Ruth says, taking a sip of her concoction.

"Yes." I shimmy out of my cover-up to get more comfortable, then lean back and moan as I sip the juice. "So good."

Ruth makes a dainty snort. "No wonder Nico is all aflutter."

I jerk my head in her direction. Nico is a-what?

Laughing, Ilaria gives a playful slap to Ruth's thigh.

Oh, so many things to say and *not* to say. Does Ilaria know he spent the night with me, but not in the fun way? Has he talked about me? He's *aflutter*? I'm rather fluttery too, if we're being honest. Pretty sure I shouldn't be that honest around Ilaria McGossiper but still, some information is meant to be shared.

I smile and sip. "He's a true gentleman."

That gets me two approving grins.

"He is," Ruth says. "You and him would make beautiful babies."

I snort the delicious juice into my nose and cough.

Ilaria presses her finger and thumb to her forehead. "Ruth."

"What?" the older woman says. "They would. I never got to be an Oma, and when I see a chance, I'm going to take it. This island has so few little ones. It's missing those tiny sparks of life and adventure."

Oma...Grandma? "Oh," I rasp, still dealing with the burning citrus in my sinuses. I sniff and try to form words around the sting. "Um. Is Nico your, uh, son?"

She lets me stew, face relaxed in amusement, waves crashing a bit closer, and clouds covering the sun, then blinking the spotlight on again.

"No," she says. "Though I treat him as one sometimes, probably to his dismay." She smiles as though that's not dismal *at all*. "But also his improvement. If he won't do, there are many others to choose from. What's your type?" She sits up and sips her drink, neck stretched and head swiveling as she scans the beach for potential suitors.

I suck the rest of my drink down so hard, the straw vibrates with my slurp. "Uh. No. I just left a long relationship, remember? Like yesterday. Before that, it was a casual high school boyfriend, then a few dates and—" How does one say "a couple of needy one-night stands" without actually saying that? "Dates." Close enough. One involved food. "I need me time."

"And you're snorkeling tomorrow with Nico," Ilaria unhelpfully tosses out into the world.

I glance at my phone's dark screen. She couldn't have read my phone, so he must have told her. Interesting. "Mm-hmm," I answer and ignore the told-you-so expression she proudly wears.

"To be young again," Ruth says. "You enjoy every one of those…dates, dear." She winks.

I caught the meaning of that one.

7

PASSER LE EMPANADA

*E*ven though I set my alarm for six forty-five to catch the sunrise, I'm up at six fifteen and making coffee. Bedtime came early last night since I went alcohol-free and didn't get much sleep the night before with the barfing, ogling Nico, and angst with James.

I needed the beach, good food, and sleep. The company of Ilaria and Ruth didn't hurt either.

My breakup wound is more of an itchy scar today—closed and healing.

A text from Nico brings a smile to my face before the initial excitement wears off. We're not dating. Sure, he's sweet and has seen me in more compromising positions than most, but a day is too soon to have a crush on someone, even a temporary one brought on from pushing away from James for a while. Maybe that's my problem—the scared part of my brain that held on because of guilt, stability, and gratitude finally caught on that the relationship was over, and Nico is the safe, sweet eye candy I've been craving. I'm on vacation and he's here, a secretive hotel owner far away from where I live. He's a perfect post-relationship flirt partner who has to be nice because I'm a guest.

He's taking me snorkeling at nine, when he says the fish are most active. It was a short message, and I didn't see him after he left yesterday. What else does he do? More specifically, who else does he do? Maybe he rejected my rebound offer because his dance card is already full. Why should that matter? It doesn't.

Seriously though, he's handsome, makes me giggle, and is the secret owner of a glorious hotel where everyone walks around in skimpy clothing, including the staff on their time off. I understand the behind-the-scenes drama of resort life. The lifeguard can't be busy all the time with arcade attendants. Nico's bedroom probably has a revolving door installed. Not that it matters.

Fa la la, fuck.

I step outside and sip coffee as the first tendrils of deep red peek over the ocean. The growing light highlights the silhouette of palms and a few people walking the beach. I bet the cool sand feels nice. There's a couple holding hands. Another snuggling in a double hammock tied between two palm trees. A group walks toward the rolling waves that kiss the shore. I can't think of a better alarm than rolling waves.

A single person leans against a palm tree. That beachy hair is familiar as well as his defined shoulders, even hidden under a long-sleeved shirt.

I toss on a sweater and a pair of shorts and carry my mug to the elevator.

The sand is indeed cool. I head toward the palm trees and step in line beside Nico but keep my eyes on the ocean. "Merry Christmas Eve."

The heat of his gaze makes me turn to glance at him.

He's smiling. "Merry Christmas Eve to you too." His voice, like mine, carries the rasp of first morning words.

I hide my giddy grin with my coffee cup, and he lifts his in cheers. His mug is stoneware, gray and earthy—not hotel-issued drinkware.

"You're hygge, Cozi," he says, tugging the chunky fabric at my elbow.

"What language?"

He licks his lips and puts his eyes back on the ocean. "Danish. Sorry. It means coziness."

"You're from Denmark?"

He won't look at me but gives a slight nod. Hmm. Why is that so uncomfortable for him?

"Well, I'm feeling...hygge." I lean against his palm tree. "Did I say that right?"

He grins as he takes a sip of coffee. "Close...ish."

"My suitcase arrived, but I didn't pay attention to what I was packing before I left the apartment." I shrug and refocus on the water. "I'm more prepared for a northern winter."

"It's a good morning for it. It's cooling off. Did you sleep well?"

"I did."

"Late night again?"

His tone forces my gaze. I can't read him. His brows are almost furrowed yet not. It's like he's having an emotion that hasn't figured out what it is yet.

I shake my head. "No. Early to bed..." I wave a hand at the lightening sky. "You?"

"Same. Healthy, wealthy, and wise...or something like that, I think it goes."

Was that a hint for me or a repeat of an old phrase?

Silence overtakes us in that tense moment seconds before the main event. Even the early seabirds shush right before a sliver of molten orange shows itself. The anticipation is worth it. Peach streaks wiggle across the sky, blending to yellow. The color is in constant motion, morphing as the sun rises inch by inch and reflects off gentle waves.

"Wow," I breathe out, holding my coffee mug to my chest.

"Mm-hmm." Nico reaches back and tucks my hair behind

my ear. His fingertips skim my skin, stirring up a tremor. He turns to the sunrise when I put my attention on him.

I can't stop the tug at the corners of my mouth. *Aflutter.*

A group lines up along the shoreline. It's a wedding. Ruth, dressed in a cream linen dress, faces the couple and holds open a book as she speaks. She didn't tell me she was a marriage officiant, though it makes sense with her job.

The party laughs, then the bride and groom slide together in a kiss. Sweet.

I glance back at the sunrise. "A couple of hours until swim time, huh? You going to show me all the fishes?"

Nico chuckles. "There will be lots of fish to chase. Are you a breakfast person?"

"Some days."

More couples wander out to stick their toes in the water and greet the morning.

Nico pushes off the palm. "Are you one today?"

"Are you asking me to breakfast?" I flutter my lashes at him.

"I can't, remember? However, it's my—*our* duty to make sure you're well taken care of, breakfast included." He tugs a lock of my hair until I swat his hand away.

"Does 'well taken care of' mean pulling my pigtails like we're on a playground?"

Nico gives some strands on the other side a quick tug, then drops his hand as I aim for that one. "Simona Island is a playground, Cozi. You'll see. Come on, my favorite chef is working today. He made empanadas."

"What's that? It's not fish, is it?" I scrunch my nose.

"No, it's a pastry of meat. You don't like fish? Vegetarian?" He settles a warm palm on the small of my back and turns me toward the hotel.

"No. I love fish, but as we're going to hang out with them, it would be in bad taste to eat them right before."

He pushes his lips out in consideration. "Somehow that's logical to me."

Ruth pops up beside me and loops her arm in mine. "Good morning, Cozette. You're looking beautiful today. Don't you think so, Nico?"

"Good morning." I grin and set my head on her shoulder for a moment. She reaches to pat my cheek.

Nico's eyes narrow the slightest bit before he puts his focus on the hotel as we move forward. "I see you two have met. Good wedding?"

She nods. "Yes. They're a lovely couple. Much like—"

"Got to get empanadas before they're gone." Nico takes my empty mug and presses it next to his in his grip. He snatches my fingers and drags me forward. "Happy Christmas Eve, Miss Ruth."

I jog to keep up, and Ruth's raspy laugh grows distant. I squeeze his hand. "Um. So..." I raise my eyebrows at him.

"She's a kind and darling pest." He releases my fingers to open the door for me. "Thinks everyone should marry in their twenties. What did you two talk about?" He's stiff and scowly. Interesting.

"Events, her husband, and how she came to the island. How she treats you like her son, though you are not." I sigh and point to my mug in his hand. "I'm going to need a refill on coffee. You're in your twenties?"

He relaxes the slightest bit and sidles up beside me. "Twenty-nine as of a few weeks ago. You?"

He's young to own a hotel resort, but I didn't know if his youthful appearance was deceptive like Ruth's.

"Happy belated birthday," I say. "I'll be twenty-six in February."

"Happy upcoming birthday."

I head to the first room on the right. The two sets of double doors are propped wide in the dining hall and the lights are low, making the chandelier sparkle with the pink sunrise coming through the two-story windows and the open-paneled wall that spills tables draped in white tablecloths out onto a tiled patio. The fireplace sparks with a gentle fire inside its dark wood enclosure.

This is a much different experience than the dim evening ambiance meant for romance. They've structured the space for a calm waking and I'm impressed. There are few guests yet. Sunrise breakfast, even on vacation, should be teeming with people. Come to think of it, this place should be busier. Packed full like the locations I checked in the States.

Maybe El Escape Azul isn't the paradise I think it is.

Nico sets our mugs on a booth table against the wall before walking toward the sounds of clinking serving spoons and early chatter. "There's the man." He points to a chef with thin, shoulder-length dreads under his tall white hat, though we already have the man's attention.

The chef waves us over, coming out from behind the line of buffets. "Bonjour," he says with a Parisian accent, and I nearly do a jig.

"Bonjour," I return. "Tu viens de Paris?"

"Oui!" He shucks off his white gloves and takes my hand in both of his. "De quelle région viens-tu?"

"North Carolina," I say. "My father left Paris when he was eight, and my mother is three generations from Marseille."

Nico's fingers skim my back again, then drop away. "Jules, meet Cozette. She's a VIP traveler, so we have to take good care of her. She came for the empanadas."

"J'ai encore mieux," Jules says, shaking his finger at Nico. "Go sit. I'll bring you a plate."

"We've got it, but thank you," Nico says and signals me toward the tables of food.

"Just as well. Busy, busy." Jules bobs his head at me. "C'était un plaisir de vous te rencontrer."

"Toi aussi," I return. It was a pleasure.

As Jules turns to go back, and I open my mouth to ask Nico why a French chef is making empanadas, I notice a woman in an El Escape Azul uniform staring at us—well, glaring from beside the kitchen entrance. She's in full makeup like she's come from a photo shoot, and when she crosses her arms, her nails sparkle like she has diamonds stuck to them. The smile that everyone else has in this magical place is missing.

Nico steps around me, crossing in the path of my view, and takes my fingers in his but then drops them. An expression of concern passes over his features, and he glances around like he's been caught stealing Santa's cookies. I peek around him, and the woman is gone.

Four days left to learn about this man I'm becoming impatient to learn about.

I lean closer. "Was that your ex?"

"No. Though she's been persistent about getting involved." He gives a little jerk and squints. I don't think he meant to say that. I like that a little too much. It puts us one step closer to even, as he's seen me in multiple uncomfortable situations.

"Oh, ho ho ho." I walk toward the first buffet table and grab a plate. "I bet I'm a better flirt." I flick my eyebrows at him and he chuckles, sending a thread of relief through me. She's not a sore point for him.

"Yes, even when you're drunk-flirting."

"Absolutely," I say, spearing a slice of melon. "I'm truthful. Coconuts are indeed edible."

"*Eatable*," Nico corrects.

"That too." No one but Dad has ever corrected me back to my pointedly incorrect words.

I need more from this man. He follows behind me, close but not close enough. I want to turn and blurt that I know he's the owner and then hug him, but he wants to keep secrets. What else does he hide and why? He should be proud of this place, even if it's not packed to the rim. It's a paradise with attentive singing concierges and wedding planners who want to bask in everyone's romance.

I browse the selection of breads. "The boss is pretty strict on that employee dating thing, huh?"

He moves closer, engulfing me in warmth as he reaches past me to nab a chocolate strawberry. It goes on my plate. "Only when it comes to guests."

"Ooh. So the staff is allowed to have all the fun." I grab a slice of pineapple carved to look like a flower. "I should apply."

He opens his mouth, then shuts it, appearing lost, so I nudge him with an elbow. "Kidding. What if I don't like chocolate?"

"You do," he says, finally finding his words.

"How do you know?"

He raises an eyebrow in response and glances back to the buffet, going starry-eyed. "Here. Empanadas." Golden half-moon pockets fill tiered servers. Little signs with too-perfect script mark chicken, beef, cheese, and apple.

"You have a French chef, yet I don't see French food?" I heat a little, because that could be taken as himself, Nico, hired the chef, which he very well could have, but I'm not supposed to—.

"You haven't been here long enough and he's a pâtissier. Everyone knows pastry chefs come from France. Geez, Cozi." He gives a dramatic eye roll.

I poke his hard side as he grins at me in a way that says if we were tumbling beyond this guest/owner flirting, he'd pinch my hip. Then I'd do something ridiculous like flick his nipple, and he'd laugh instead of taking offense, and we'd poke some more. And kiss. Feeding each other strawberries after tracing chilled chocolate lines over—.

I haven't answered. I clear my throat and move along the line. "Hey now. Be kind to naïve VIP guests. I was wondering why the bread was so good. Those biscuits yesterday..."

"Those biscuits." He closes his eyes and gives a hum of bliss. "You should have his crème anything. He makes me a Koldskål that is better than any I've ever had." His eyes meet mine, and there's a hint of shock and fear in them.

He's getting comfortable with me. I smile. "Maybe he will make crème something before the week is up."

Nico nods and follows as we finish filling our plates and sit at the table claimed with our mugs. A carafe of steaming coffee and a tiny pitcher of foamy cream sit next to a small, clear vase filled with a bright crimson hibiscus.

With Nico eyeing me in anticipation, I taste the empanada. Salt and savory spices. Crisped shell filled with melt-in-your-mouth meat. It's like pie and tacos met and had the most glorious love child. I moan. "That is the best."

Nico lights up and dives in.

"So you grew up in Denmark?"

His happy demeanor crashes into a look of shock and fear. He clears his throat. "Yes. I moved here four years ago."

That explains the accent. "But visited before that. I can understand why. It's amazing here. Though that's quite an adjustment."

He nods. "What's North Carolina like?"

Slick subject change there, Nico. I take a bite of melon to try to tame my expression.

I tell him about growing up in North Carolina, my parents, my high school friends who are all still there. While he doesn't say much about himself, he does relax. For a while longer I can be patient. I'm only here a few days. I shouldn't push someone to share who clearly isn't ready. Besides, I'm here for me, not him. No matter how handsome he is, or that he can't seem to stop touching me, or how much I like his eyes, especially when they're focused on me.

We walk from the dining hall, and the glaring woman from earlier strides toward us. Nico stalls a step, then out of a hallway pops Ilaria, who nabs the woman and drags her away, whisper-yelling a string of Spanish words.

Nico walks forward again as if Ilaria didn't just divert the Grinch from Santa and his bag of presents. "Do you know Spanish?" he asks quietly.

"Nope."

"Good."

I bite back a laugh.

Ilaria raises a finger in front of Miss Grinch's face and points down a hall. The woman sends a glare my way and stomps out of sight. Knowing Ilaria, I'll hear about that by lunch.

Nico halts at the elevator and turns to me.

"Are you sleeping with her?" I blurt out before he can speak, then full-wince—one eye squinted and everything. Sleigh bells, my tongue is untamable.

His eyebrows raise way up, but he smiles and then relaxes. This time he twirls one of my locks. "No. Never. Even when she took all her clothes off and threw herself on my bed."

My mouth drops open, and he shuts it with a finger on my chin.

"Yep," he says, popping the P. "That's Ilaria's niece." He frowns and clasps his hands behind his back. "Sorry. That was unprofessional. Um, will you meet me in the lobby in a half hour?"

I want him to share, professionalism be damned. If he knew half the secrets spilled in the drunken late-night VIP lounges during any event, he would realize one naked person trying to get in his pants is called a Friday. "Sure." I turn toward the elevator, push the button, and turn back to hug him. "I'm sorry that happened to you. That has to be awkward."

His arms wrap tight around me, and I swear his nose brushes the top of my head. That's confirmed when the heat of his exhale tickles me. "Thank you." His voice sounds almost...relieved.

The ding pulls me away from him and the doors swing open. He watches me and sugarplums dance in my stomach, then slump back into slumber the second the doors close.

Maybe I've misjudged him. Being the owner has to be difficult for him, with women pursuing him. Not that they wouldn't if he just drove the van. He's one of those rare presents that shocks you with its awesomeness when you get a glimpse inside. Still, was she so blatant about her wants because he's who he is, or because of *what* he is?

I've seen it before, the way some people throw themselves at the boss. I never did, which is why I went so far in my position. You don't let yes-men run events. They'd get trampled with requests, give everything away, and walk out with nothing but exhaustion and worn-through shoes—not that I didn't eventually get there. My break was for different reasons. When you deal in the upper echelon, motives and actions mean everything. If you stand up for the things you need, stay in clear communication, and keep emotion out of it, everything is smooth sailing.

I huff a laugh as the elevator doors open. The irony between my personal life and business life has never been so obvious.

8

SHARK BAIT

*N*ico pulls the van off the road at a red-painted stick pointing out of the ground in front of a forest of trees and brush. We travel on a flattened sand path between two rows of thick palms.

We drove less than ten minutes from El Escape, but thick dark-green underbrush billows beneath thick trees draped with vines, and reeds poke out of the sand instead of the hotel's manicured flowers and groomed beach.

"Off-roading?" I ask, leaning forward to check out the wild surroundings.

"Only for a moment."

His cryptic clues about where we're going and what we will encounter are delightfully irritating. I'm on the edge of my seat. Well, as far as I can be with the seat belt holding me back. Are we going to a secret marina for a boat? How far will we have to travel? He said he likes to kayak, which explains those shoulders and pectorals. Maybe we will do that too. If you dive from a kayak, can you get back in?

We pop out of the tropical forest to see a tiny pink house with a red-tiled patio. My apartment—James's apartment in

New York may be bigger. A brown dog with one perked-up ear raises its head and lumbers to its feet. It barks once and ambles toward the van as Nico pulls to a stop and steps out, grabbing the paper bag of aluminum tins from behind the console. He says something in Spanish, and the dog wags its tail and makes chirpy little whines as Nico cups its muzzle and plants a kiss on its head.

O holy night, he likes dogs.

He glances at me over his shoulder while scratching the dog's head. "I'll be one second, maybe three."

He jogs across the sand and across the patio as the door opens and a white-haired man with a cane leans out the door, a wide, mustached smile on his wrinkled face. They grasp each other's shoulders and the man waves him inside, but Nico shakes his head and says something that makes the man laugh and glance in the way of the van. I wave, and the older man returns the gesture, knobby fingers spread wide, then gives Nico's cheek a pat. They chat another moment before Nico passes over the bag and strolls back to the van.

"He seems nice," I say as he pops the van in drive and bumps along on the sand.

"Mm-hmm."

I wait for him to explain, but he heads behind the house where a beach awaits. It's empty except for a small group of birds fighting over a crab.

"Not telling me about the gentleman in the pink house, then?"

He beams at me. "I was wondering if you would ask." Then he goes silent again.

I glare at the side of his face. "So, what's with the gentleman in the pink house?"

"Who?"

"Nico!" I yell-laugh and swat his shoulder.

"That's Angel, and he loves that pink house."

I roll my hand through the air.

"Oh, you want more?" He blinks with feigned innocence. "His dog's name is Caterina, Cat for short, and she's fifteen." His expression is smug, as if he'd settled all questions about the mysterious driveway, palm forest, and food delivery to the old man in the pink house.

"You're getting coal for Christmas." I cross my arms and lean back in my seat.

He laughs and stops the van. "I'd need to be way naughtier to deserve coal." He leans closer, eyeing my lips. My whole body lights up like he flipped the switch on a Christmas tree. Then he tucks that lip under his teeth, and I want to punch him then kiss him. Maybe kiss him then punch him. Whatever, I want to kiss him.

I move until we're inches apart. His lip pops out from under his teeth, expression sliding from jest to something more serious.

"You're getting coal in your stocking, you tease." I jerk the door handle and hop out of the van, feet sinking into warm sand. The beach is quiet except for the van doors slamming. The sound sends a few of the fighting birds on their way.

He holds out a blue-rimmed mask and snorkel. "We're here."

It doesn't look like much, just sand and shoreline. Waves roll over the rock and shell-lined shore, and I'm pretty sure that El Escape Azul rakes their beach. I'm not sure which I like better. El Escape is paradise, but this location is real. It's homey —a living room that has kids toys scattered and a dog on the couch. You're not afraid to touch stuff or put your feet on the coffee table.

"It's fantastic." I tug my T-shirt off and take the mask from Nico, looping the strap over my arm while I braid my hair.

He watches me as he opens the van's side door and drags his shirt off as well. "Yeah?"

"Yes. Really pretty." I'd tell him that the natural beauty is almost better, but I don't want to insult his hotel, even though it would be tough to find fault in El Escape.

I keep quiet, attempting to drag my eyes from his abs and the sharp dip in his sides, but they're stuck. I want to explore. Run fingers over every muscle to see what they feel like and how he responds to my touch. Would he tense or relax? Moan or growl? I unbutton my shorts and wiggle out of them.

Nico makes an approving hum, leaning against the van. His blatant, unashamed staring is so normal to me, it's eerie. Maybe it's because I ogle him as much as he ogles me. Excellent. We're perfectly compatible oglers.

I need to dip in a cold ocean. Blowing out a breath, I put the mask over my head and adjust the strap. Nico comes closer and rolls into his El Escape guest safety speech for masks, flippers, swimming in currents, and not touching coral, all while adjusting my mask, making sure it has a seal around my face.

"Got it?" he asks with a tilted-head smile. "You're cute in that."

I poke his side and barely refrain from returning to him with more fingers, my palm, my lips. "I need a fraternizing alarm."

That gets me a raised eyebrow and lip nibble as he grabs two sets of flippers from the van and starts walking. The back view of him is nearly as good as the front, and I need to chill. He glances back at me since I'm stuck still, busy staring at his ass, defined calves, and low-slung swim trunks that show off the dimples above his hips. He turns a circle, looking confused for a moment until I laugh, then he grins wide, returns to snatch my hand, and drags me where soft, dry footing turns cool and firm. He tugs his mask on and walks into a wave. "It's mostly sand and shell here, until we get to the reef, but starfish too, so be careful where you step. Follow me."

The warm water surrounds my ankles and then a bigger

wave hits and knocks me back a step. I squeak and Nico tugs me out with him. Once we breach the line of breaking waves, gentle ripples only come up to my chest, and he hands me a pair of flippers.

I can see the sand below my feet—shells and I dodged one starfish—but the ocean is vast, and a little panic hits me, making me stall and glance back at the safety of dry land thirty feet away.

Nico tugs at my hand. "You ready to go under?"

I chew my lip.

"Are you freaking out right now?" He tilts his head.

"Only a little." I shrug. "Big ocean. Bitey fish. You know."

"I do. Face down, come on."

He pushes off the sand to dunk his head and drags me forward. Once my face is under the surface and I adjust to breathing through the snorkel, the world turns into silent fantasy.

The water is clear and quiet, except for the blue of the distant deep. A line of short seagrass leads to rough gray and black-veined rock and tan coral. Hundreds of fish in a rainbow of colors dart in and out of crater hidey-holes and wiggle around pastel anemone.

I squeal through my snorkel.

Nico guides me over to a mini-reef. I have to be careful not to kick, because some of the areas are close to the surface of the water. A group of cellphone-sized black fish stick close to a bumpy coral structure with two giant leaves sticking out of the side. It looks like a bumpy beret with collard green feathers.

Darting down for a closer look, Nico points out a clump of red. I take a deep breath and submerge. It's a cuddle puddle of tiny red starfish with spindly arms. I squeeze Nico's shoulder in thanks, then a big orange and turquoise striped fish with prominent rounded-off teeth catches my attention. It eyes us warily as we approach and backs away between two rocks.

When I run out of air, I swim to the surface and pull my snorkel. Nico's right beside me.

"What was that?" I ask, grinning so hard my face hurts.

Nico tugs his mouthpiece to the side. "Triggerfish. Gorgeous, right?"

I squeal. "Amazing! And the starfish. Geez, and the feathered beret!"

Nico tilts his head as I jam the salt-tinged plastic mouthpiece in, take a deep breath, and dive. Some of the bigger fish get brave and come to visit. I wiggle my fingers at a yellow one, and he nibbles on me. He gives up when he realizes I'm not delicious and then moves up to taste my face mask, his sucker mouth landing right between my eyes. The air bubbles from my laughter send him darting away, and I have to resurface for air.

I wanted adventure, and here I am. How could I have ever been remotely frightened of this enchanting place? Though it's Christmas, I make a New Year's resolution: Don't be scared of new things. Especially when those new things involve swimming around in a massive natural aquarium.

As we make our way parallel to the coast, Nico grabs my arm and points. A school of tiny silver fish flash like a row of dimes, then scatter, revealing a speckled-brown octopus climbing across the coral. We follow it as its arms sprawl, grabbing to drag itself along in a graceful walk.

I watched *The Blue Planet* once and was amazed at the life under the sea, but witnessing these creatures firsthand is surreal.

Breaching once again, I find myself alone at the surface. I take in gulps of air. Nico still hasn't come up.

I tread holding my mouthpiece, when he pops up near the sand area, making a huge splash. There's a huge starfish on his face. He holds onto it with both hands and yells a muffled cry that sounds like my name behind the pale orange creature.

I scream, "Nico!" and swim over when he lowers the starfish back to the water, lifts his mask, and smiles wide.

"Ah, you asshole!" I yell and splash him.

He laughs and lunges to catch me around the waist with one arm, holding the submerged creature in his other hand as it overflows his palm like a star-shaped dinner plate.

"So much coal!" I punch his shoulder, and he tugs me closer to his side. My fist relaxes and I palm his chest, entwine one leg around his, and let him hold me up, feet not touching the sand. The heat of his skin makes the surrounding water downright chilly.

"Look," he says, balancing me and bringing the starfish closer, but keeping it underwater. "This is a red cushion sea star. It's an omnivore native to the Atlantic Ocean. We have a lot of them in this area."

The sea star is thick and pale orange and has a line of short, cream-colored nubs lining each of its five legs. It's so symmetrical, it doesn't seem real.

"You can touch," Nico whispers.

He holds still as I move my hand from his chest and dip my fingers under the water. It's smooth and slightly spongy, like a leather chair.

"It's not as hard as I thought it would be," I say, leaning to study it.

Nico chuckles and I press the side of its arm. It gives resistance, trying to push me away, but it doesn't have the power to do so.

"Aw, it's trying to escape, I think," I say.

"Should we turn it loose?"

"Yeah. Let him live his happy sea star life."

Nico smiles. "Hold your breath."

I drag on the mask, and he drops us into the water, settling the sea star into the sand next to a smaller one.

We pop back up, and he shakes his head, sending sprays of

sea water walloping the plastic in front of my eyes like heavy rain against a windshield. I squeal and struggle, but he keeps his arm firmly around my waist. I'd call a fraternization alarm again, but I'm afraid he'd stop. I lift my mask, and Nico traces the indentation on my cheek.

"Are you having fun?" he asks, quiet and serious.

"I am. I think you might be five-star."

That brings back his grin. "Oh yeah. Might?" He moves closer, and the ideas he has about crossing the lines with guests lays somewhere back on the beach.

He's going to kiss me.

His finger moves from my cheek to my chin, and his nose brushes mine, sending sweet flurries on a whirlwind around my stomach.

Something bumps my leg, and I turn to see a big fucking fin. Like a dun-dun fin.

"Shark!" I scream and flail. "Shark. Sharksharkshark—"

"Cozi," Nico says, entirely too calm.

I climb him, and he laughs as the fin continues on and turns back toward us again. The shadow surrounding the fin is eat-people big. I've draped my leg over his shoulder, and I'm holding onto his head. My other leg is in the chow zone, but most of Nico is as well. Why is he standing here, laughing? Shark.

Not good, not good. Not. Good.

"Cozi," Nico singsongs. He oomphs and sidesteps when I flail to get to higher ground.

"Shark!" I yell louder.

"Uh-huh." To my utter horror, he reaches out as the fin comes closer.

Instead of taking off his hand, the shark slides by as Nico's fingers sweep over its back, then it turns again. It's as big as I am.

I make some kind of gasping sound of confusion. "But...but—"

"Yes, it's a shark. A nurse shark. She won't hurt you. See the tag?"

Sure enough, there's a pale blue square with black numbers stuck to the fin like an earring.

"Does that mean she's genetically mutated to only eat kelp and algae?"

He tugs at my leg. "No. That's just Bonnie. She's been visiting this location for decades. The nurse sharks aren't hunting this time of day. Come down, and don't flop around. Gentle movements."

"But...shark?"

"Yes, she's a shark. No bitey though." His thumb sweeps back and forth over my thigh. "Seriously, it's okay," he says in laughing spurts.

I reluctantly let go of his forehead and slide until I'm piggyback, legs latched around his waist. The shark moves closer, and Nico pries my hand from his shoulder and exhales a "shh." He links our fingers and reaches for her. *A shark.* Her skin is wet velvet as she glides by, unfazed by touch, or possibly even enjoying the attention.

As she comes back around, Nico tugs me in front of him, encompassing me like a heated wall, then extends my hand. I giggle as my fingers brush over her whole body. "Oh my wow," I whisper and grin.

"You're so stunned," he says against my ear. "You forgot what time of year it was."

"Huh?" I ask, glancing at him.

He sweeps wet strands of hair behind my ear. "You didn't curse something Christmassy."

"Oh." I turn back to watch Bonnie circle around. "Yeah, I am... festive. My parents are the same way. I've grown up with decorations for every holiday." Were it up to me, the New York apartment's halls would have been seriously decked. "My next place, wherever that is, will be Santa's workshop worthy next year."

"I like that about you."

My cheeks heat, and I pull my mask back down to hide. "You should see me around St. Patrick's Day." I throw on my Irish accent. "Blarney stone, that's a pot o' gold-sized shark." For a split second, a flash of nervousness smashes into me. That was the type of over-the-top that people firmly embedded in my life get. I expect furrowed brows or even an eye roll, but Nico laughs at my silliness.

"So creative," he says. "Every holiday, huh?"

I can't hold back my grin. "Yeah. Can I swim with her?" I want to see her without the barrier of choppy water, and I need to tamp down an overdose of feelings I'm unsure what to do with yet.

"That's the way." Nico pushes me away. "She's big. That's really apparent under the water, and there are others, though they tend to stay farther out, okay?"

"Okay."

A little nervous chill goes through me, but when she passes, I dunk under the water and follow. Nico wasn't exaggerating. Her smooth gray skin looks soft under the water, and she's far bigger than I am. When she rounds again, I swim backward but bump into Nico. He wraps an arm around me, and the heat of him settles me. After a moment I even think she's kinda cute with her small, oval mouth and fleshy mustache.

We touch her side as she passes, and then he kicks off and releases me. We swim next to her. She takes a relaxing swim through the water as if she has all the time in the world.

I guess there's not much to do as a shark but eat and swim. It sounds delightful except for the lack of Christmas decorations.

We follow Bonnie out into the reef, watching her graceful

glide. The other fish don't appear bothered by her, though they don't leave the safety of their natural city on the sandy floor. She must not be hungry. I pause in the water when the dark bodies of a bunch of nurse sharks contrast against the blue water. They meander in a circulating school throughout twenty feet of water. Nico taps me and points up. I pop up, spit out the snorkel, and tread water.

He pulls his mouthpiece aside and smiles. "We don't have to go out there, but it's really fun to swim with them. They're much smaller than Bonnie, because I think most of them are her kids."

"Aw," I coo. "Her babies? I want to."

I never thought I'd be swimming with sharks that actually seem sweet. Who gets to do that on Christmas Eve? *Me.* I get to do that on Christmas Eve, and I'm shaking like a holly leaf with excitement.

Nico chuckles and nods. "Okay. Remember, smooth movements. And don't grab them or put your limbs close to their mouths. They may bunch around you, so if you start to panic, gently push them in another direction and work your way back to shallow water."

"Okay." I rapidly bob my head and shove my snorkel back in place.

Nico stays close as we approach the group, then dives down, swimming through about ten of them. They are only about three feet long. A couple are bigger, but Bonnie stands out. She swings back by me, and I slide my fingertips along her body.

Nico focuses on one, following it until he holds it in place, examining it. I dive and peek over his shoulder. There's a bite taken out of the small shark's fin. Aw. Poor baby. Nico lets it go, and it darts off, as fast as a nurse shark can. It doesn't seem to have any problems swimming.

Nico surfaces, blowing the water from his snorkel. I follow and then we dive together. The little sharks surround us, seeming to accept us as one of them, curiously approaching, then hanging out with us. I match their speed, floating along as I study the differences in each. Some are slightly darker, a few have scars. One has a much longer fleshy mustache and darker eyes. Must be the bad guy.

After more surface visits for air, Nico takes my hand and tugs me back to the reef.

He pulls his mask up. "Want to head in for lunch?"

"No, I want to stay here forever. What time is it?"

He glances at a nice watch on his wrist I hadn't noticed before. "After one."

"Kris Kringle, we've been out here a long time."

"Okay, say bye to the shark babies."

I flip my mask on and dunk my head underwater. "Bye, babies." My yell is a line of bubbles. "Bye, Bonnie."

Nico is laughing when I pop out of the water. I'll come back and visit the island again, I think. I'd want to see the fish and sharks, and Nico. It already stings my chest to think about getting back on an airplane and heading back to the States.

He treads water, closer. "It's fun, isn't it?"

"I love it! This was amazing."

"Five-star amazing?"

I move closer and kiss him on the cheek. "I'd give six if I could."

His hand settles on the small of my back, grazing my bikini bottoms and keeping me close. Bonnie glides by again, and Nico runs his knuckles over her back. "I didn't expect her to be here with the storm rolling in. I would have warned you."

I run a finger over her dorsal fin. "There's a storm?"

His brows furrow. "There's a hurricane scheduled to hit land tomorrow afternoon."

9

YULETIDE GAMES

My eyes pop wide at the mention of a hurricane, and my previous fear of sharks is now no big deal. "Seriously? How in the hell did I not know this?" I wade toward the beach, fighting the resistance of receding waves and awkwardly navigating with flippers. I jerk them off my feet and hold them high as I stomp against the current. "There should be, like, a bulletin board or something in the lobby saying, 'You should have stayed in the snow, because on this island, a hurricane's gonna blow!'"

"You really didn't know?" Nico says behind me. "I, uh, did not mean to rhyme that. Look, it's rare this time of year and already slowing, so it will probably turn into a tropical storm, but we announced it. Hey, hold up."

I trip over a wave, but Nico catches me and spins me to face him. "Are you scared?"

"No!" Yes. Absolutely.

"Cozi," he says with a you're-lying accentuation.

I glare at him because he can read me and I can't always do the same, because the man avoids talking about himself.

He sighs and holds my hand, tugging me through a wave. "Never been in a hurricane, then?"

"I'm from the west part of North Carolina. The most weather we get is rain and lawn chair-tumbling gusts when the coast gets hit with something."

"It will be okay. We prepare the hotel for storms. It's only three years old, and it has the highest quality of building materials."

It's new because the first building was taken out by *a what*? Yep, a flippin' hurricane. The van driver is familiar with the building supplies because he's the flippin' owner of the hotel. I bite my tongue to keep from yelling that fact at him and asking him too many questions about El Escape and himself.

This secret feels heavier than it should, but he's keeping secrets too. Not that sharing matters to him. I'm just a guest leaving in a few days—if I'm not swept out to sea by a hurricane.

He drags me against him as soon as we step on dry sand, and I bury my face in the crook of his neck.

"The staff of El Escape has been through many hurricanes," he whispers. "We will keep you safe. When the prediction came on Friday, we contacted all future guests."

"My travel agent booked Saturday," I tell his jugular.

"Ah. Yeah, they should have been told. I'll talk to Ilaria."

"No. It's okay." The salty scent of him is far too calming. "It's just weird that I'm hearing about it now. Why is no one talking about it?"

He shifts his arm to give my wet braid a gentle tug. "Would you like to go on a vacation where everyone is talking about a hurricane? They know it's coming, they decided to stay, so they will avoid thinking about it until it's closer. And the staff has been through many."

I know. "Everything makes more sense now though with the guests."

"What does?" His hand travels my bare lower back, sending my skin into excited chills.

If I keep pressing myself against him and breathing him in, we'll end up rolling around in the sand and while I've never experienced it, I've heard that getting sexy on a beach isn't as fantastic as it sounds. Tiny grains of abrasive sand aren't meant for sensitive areas, and I'm not interested in that level of exfoliation, even with Nico. Maybe with Nico.

I unwind from him and drag off the mask that's perched on the top of my head. "El Escape is fantastic. It wasn't full like the other places I checked in the States. Once I got here, that didn't make sense." Grinning, I step toward the van. "I thought management may be a hot mess."

He gasps, catches up, and pinches my side. "I'm going to tell Ilaria you said that."

Ilaria, huh? "No, don't. She's wonderful." My stomach rumbles. "Holly berries, I'm so hungry."

"It sneaks up when you're distracted by the fish." He opens the van, wraps a towel around me, and hands me a water bottle. "You did well today. You played with sharks."

"I didn't expect that." I nibble my lip, and he walks around the front of the van. "That was so fun."

"I like showing you new things. Your face lights up." He pauses as he opens the door. "It's refreshing."

He lives on a resort island where most are visitors. I can't be special when it comes to the people here. We're all borrowing new landscapes and experiences that push us out of our normal and let us trip into wide-eyed amazement. But what is new to Nico? I crave a hint of his normal.

"Is that uncommon?" I ask. "I would think those you brought here would be all sparkly at what's out there."

The cloudy sky outside the window is dark in the distance. Our ocean playground is choppy. He grips the wheel, brows furrowed, not starting the van yet. "Yes. Well, no but..." He pushes the ignition button and looks at me. "You absorb it all like a sponge, and your light grows bigger whether it's learning a dance, tasting an empanada, or petting a shark. You seem to appreciate having experiences over..." His lips tighten, and he flicks his fingers through the air like he can't even say "stuff" or "money." "And that's what is rare."

Is it? My parents are the same way. "I'd rather do something than have something," I say. "Unless it's a pair of Jimmy Choos and then..." I display my hands like "what's a girl to do," then laugh at his frown, leaning way over to rub my finger against the wrinkle between his brows until he grins at me. Mission accomplished, I settle firmly back in my seat and do not crawl over the console to straddle his lap. Nope. "I'd definitely choose a trip like this over many things. I haven't been able to be adventurous in a while. Wasn't planning on being adventurous with a hurricane though."

He drives toward the pink house and waves as the curtains in the front window flutter and a hand pokes out to bid farewell. "Will he be okay in the storm?" I ask.

Nico brushes his knuckles over my upper arm. "He's been in that house for sixty of his ninety-five years. He'll be fine."

"Sixty?" I look back at the house. It's sturdy enough, but for a hurricane?

"He's thinking about moving to an assisted living home in the spring. Says the summer is too hot, but I think he's lonely and it's getting harder to move around." He drums a beat on the steering wheel. "Do you have a dog?"

Nico, king of the subject change.

"My grandmother is in assisted living. She loves it. They have Friday movie night and Taco Tuesday. Her beta fish is quite happy there as well." I keep my elbows on the chair rests but wish the seats were closer. I'd press my arm against his on the console, but there's a foot of space between the seats. "And I don't have any pets, though I love dogs. I possibly even love nurse sharks now. Did you go to college in Denmark?"

"Europe. Was your first job in North Carolina?"

I chew my cheek. Okay, so he still doesn't share, and maybe I didn't chatter as much as I thought I did on rum punch night. Is it okay that I don't know much about him and that his idea of details is to give me the answer of *Europe*? It is, I think. I'm not here for him, and maybe he needs time. But I'm down to four days, three nights, two Christmas present ideas, and one hurricane in a palm tree. *Enjoy the moment, Cozette.*

Alright. I will be merry and bright, and I will be me. He can be him, and then I will leave. Simple is good.

He brushes his fingers over my hand, slowing the van. "Are you okay?"

Let the yuletide games begin.

"Yes, sorry. I was distracted by..." I wave my hand at the surrounding jungle. "What did you ask? Oh, career-land. Yes, I was picked up by a company two hours from my hometown. What's your favorite Christmas song?"

He glances at me, and his pout blooms into a grin. "'Jingle Bells...the Batman smells version."

A too-loud laugh bursts from me. "I love that one too. It's not my favorite though." I fall silent and let him experience the tension of unanswered questions for once.

The van moves forward, bouncing over mini sand-dirt dunes. "It's Deck the Halls, isn't it?"

My jaw drops.

"Yes!" He beams and slaps the steering wheel. "You hum it a lot. It's a favorite Christmas curse too."

Isn't he observant. A brown furball leaps from one tree to another and I gasp. "Is that a freaking monkey?"

"Ugh, monkeys," Nico groans.

"It *is* a monkey!" I roll down the window and poke my head out.

Nico tugs me back in by my towel. "All parts inside the van, remember?"

"Rule follower."

He grins. "They like to throw things. Like poo."

I roll the window back up.

When we arrive back at El Escape, there are stacks of tarps and stuffed canvas bags where Nico parks. When I pause too long, he says, "Stakes to support the trees and to cover the flower beds." We walk toward the front on a sandstone path. "They won't go on until the last minute."

"So organized. You all really have done this before."

"Yes." His warm fingers trace over the small of my back, right above the towel wrapped around my waist. "You're in good hands."

An older, stocky man piles sandbags next to the entrance doors. "Happy holidays, Mr. Clausen," he says with a wave.

Nico stiffens, gives a small wave, and continues on.

Mr. Clausen, huh? Nicolai Clausen.

"It's a nice name," I whisper.

He opens his mouth, then shuts it again. With a gentle grasp to my forearm, he halts me. "Cozi. I—"

The workers and guests in the lobby cheer and clap, moving to circle us. Nico and I glance around at grinning faces. Did we win something? The main front desk attendant, Jennifer, points up to a ball of mistletoe hanging from the lobby light fixture and does a wiggle, grinning lips open in a silent, *Ah ha.*

I laugh.

"Oh, chestnuts," Nico says and takes a step away from me, staring at the mystical plant of kissy times. Actually, he may make a run for it.

"You're seriously not going to kiss me?" I tease. "That rule thing is super ingrained, huh?" I eye his parted lips as he looks over the circled-in crowd. He's probably scouting an opening for escape.

The chanting begins. "Kiss her. Kiss her. Kiss her."

Nico glares, but his emerging smile offsets the warning.

"Fine." I shrug. "I'll kiss you."

I step forward, fist the front of his shirt, and go up on tiptoes to peck his lips, too quick for him to kiss me back or for me to ponder the warmth or texture. As I step back and cross my arms, the group laughs more than they cheer. It was a lame kiss, but enough to shock Nico. He stands stock-still, lips slightly puckered. It's as if I created a reverse fairy tale and froze him into place instead of releasing him from a spell.

Walking backward, I head toward the elevator. "I'm going to shower off the eau-du-shark, and then lunch."

He springs to life, catching up. "Yeah. Uh, sorry about that. I forgot about the mistletoe."

It's nice to be on this side of the tease. "I'm glad you did. Now I know where to hang out."

He bites at his bottom lip, but not in that mischievous way, and studies the floor. He's uncomfortable. I wanted to lay a real kiss on him, but whatever is happening between us isn't working for him. He took me out today though, and dropped me right smack in the middle of an adventure, and for that I will be forever grateful.

"Thank you again for today," I say. "Are you working tomorrow?"

His focused gaze jerks up to my eyes. He shakes his head. "Probably prepping in the morning for the storm, but no."

The storm. "Okay. Maybe I can help, or we can catch up sometime?" Staying busy will keep me from freaking out. Hopefully.

He adds a head tilt and a deep furrow between his eyebrows, making me as confused as he looks. He exhales a long breath. "Go to lunch with me."

Huh. I tuck my towel tighter around me. "Thought you couldn't ask out the guests?"

"I didn't ask," he tosses over his shoulder, heading toward the back doors. "See you in thirty."

That's it, I have to find coal. I turn toward the elevator.

10

WRONG CLICK

A shower after ocean snorkeling is like hot cocoa after playing in the snow—necessary rejuvenation.

Skin-softening botanicals wash away the sticky layer of dried salt. I can't believe I touched a shark. Nico almost kissed me. I'm aware when a man looks at me, and Nico is constantly taking in his fill, but then pulls away. Why? Also, as boisterous as he is, he's a master at staying silent. Why, times two?

Maybe he's from a string of bad business deals. Or he's really a mafia warlord in hiding. Oh! Or he's a shunned Danish duke, banished from his homeland because...because of...

I'm being ridiculous again. He's been living on this island of rotating people. I bet that's it. Why would he get involved in personal stuff when the person he's eyeing will be gone in days? Because it's fun, feels good, and he wants to? But then after, with the goodbyes and awkward, and what if it's bad? I mean, at least I'd be leaving but still. Bad rebound holiday sex would be a memory to avoid. Maybe I should learn from him. This is a fleeting moment, and I'm here to adventure and warm up to single me again.

Besides, Nico is too sweet to get banished or be a mafia

warlord. At least I think so. Yeah, he's secretive, but he's kind, right? He takes food to ninety-five-year-olds and kisses dogs. A vision of Nico paying off the old man to hide bodies on his private beach plays through my mind. Maybe the tins were full of money.

I brush out my wet hair. I should dry it.

My laptop sits on the table, staring at me. A computerized voice says, "Are we going to do this or what?"

I shouldn't. I gnaw on the inside of my cheek. It would be wrong.

But what if I just kissed the ultimate Grinch and didn't know it? At least it was a peck. It didn't count—not really. None of my business.

Nicolai Clausen.

Click.

Images bombard the screen of a young Nico. He's adorable, even though he looks sullen and pouty. Just a teenager with shorter, slicked hair and stuffed into suits with striped ties.

Only a few photo tags are in English. *Nicolai Clausen emancipated at fourteen.*

He was legally separated from his family? A few photos further down the page are of him older, hair still short. His suits fit his wider shoulders and taper to his frame. A woman in sparkly dresses and a blunt, dark-red bob hangs on his shoulder, a pursed-lip smirky pout aimed directly at the camera in each photo. He's smiling in some, but not the crinkle-eyed full beam I've seen. Seeing past him feels so intrusive, and I put my hand on the top of my laptop to close it when I catch a headline over a photo of him with a tense jaw and narrowed eyes.

Elizabeth Marsden's tell-all pulled before publication due to defamation and invasion of privacy lawsuit.

That raises my eyebrows.

I should not be doing this. It massively violates trust. Kinda. He doesn't know I'm aware that he owns the hotel, and I've proven to myself and Ilaria that I am capable of keeping secrets. And I'm a guest—a temporary blip in his life.

That's enough to make me click again.

Just once. Once is all it takes.

I read with my hand over my mouth.

Elizabeth Marsden's tell-all book, MY BROKEN BILLIONAIRE, has been pulled from production following a lawsuit from the legal team of ex-fiancé, Nicolai Clausen. Read the premise of Marsden's attempted first publication below...

In MY BROKEN BILLIONAIRE, Elizabeth Marsden will deliver you into the rocky life of Nicolai Clausen, the only child of the screen and stage actor, Emil Clausen, and biotechnology heiress Reina Johannsson, wife and victim in the Johannsson-Clausen murder-suicide case.

At fourteen, the heir to the Clausen fortune became Denmark's youngest minor granted emancipation after an abusive year under the care of his great-uncle, who took Clausen into his home only to gain access to the minor's fortune.

After a five-year roller-coaster relationship, Marsden comes clean about Clausen's childhood, wild teen years, a secret paternity dispute, legal battles, and the heart-wrenching end to a relationship she thought would last forever.

The author's photo smiles back at me, full beam, calling me out because she knows I'm interested in diving right into the juicy secret bits of Nico's life.

I'm the worst person in the world. Well, right after this heinous bitch.

I slam my laptop shut and ball my fists in my lap. *Bad idea.* It was wrong to search. Wrong to have poked around in his publicized, difficult life. I have five minutes to pull myself together and meet with a man who is not mafia...probably, who doesn't want to be judged for his swimwear wardrobe, and who doesn't like sales calls because that's more people wanting a piece of his wallet.

If that little slice of Nico's life is somewhat true, he has damn good reason to hide away on Simona Island and drive a van like any normal guy.

I rub my forehead and head to the bathroom. New game plan. Make Nico's Christmas a great one. No more asking about private life things. He's not going to tell me and that's okay. I wouldn't tell anyone either if my ex-fiancé wrote a book about me. He was engaged? Geez. No kid should have spent their teenage years betrayed over and over. Does he have a kid?

Poor Nico.

No, I can't think that way. That's probably another reason he doesn't tell people. He's a grown man and has probably dealt with it to the best of his billionaire ability.

Yeah, he definitely doesn't need his swimwear judged.

I'm no longer hungry with the guilt filling my gut, but I swipe on lip balm, let my damp hair decide on its own style, and head downstairs.

The urgency to bolt flares brightly when I see him so he doesn't somehow peer into my brain and realize what I've done. His smile is more confident now though, and he takes my hand, entwining our fingers.

Through lunch, I find out he loves sci-fi and hates being cold. He scrunched his nose at my love of brussels sprouts, and I did the same at his affinity for eggplant. While I'm not proud of prying, I now understand the topics to avoid. Even though they're North Pole-sized topics, the conversation becomes easier. He backpacked for a year before he arrived on Simona Island the first time. He'd heard about it from an eighty-year-old man biking across South America when they ended up at the same ceviche street vendor. When Nico is free to speak about something, he is captivating. His eyes go wider, brimming with enthusiasm, and his hands signal stories in the air, painting a picture of winding rural roads, handmade art he'd wished he'd had room for, and how wide rainforest trees are now when they sprouted two thousand years ago.

I share all the places I'd like to go eventually and how I'd planned to travel overseas when I was eighteen, starting with a visit back to France, but by myself for the first time. Before I had a chance to book tickets, I received a job offer. *The* job offer. He reaches over to squeeze my hand and tells me he's sorry I chose Simona Island to start traveling. At my worried expression, he breaks into a huge grin.

"Nowhere else is as good as Simona Island," he says. "I know. I've been out there. It's why I came back to stay."

I tap my water glass against his. "I believe you."

He makes the mistake of asking what I would do for events at a place like this as we walk the property. Scavenger hunts, training events, and inviting unique specialists in yoga, parasailing, art, and YouTube star meet-and-greets all roll out in a blizzard of ideas. On the conversation of arts and crafts for adults, I tell him we should hold a cookie decorating event tomorrow afternoon for guests, and he drags me into a garden pagoda to type away on his phone. I nudge him as we're stepping through a winding path between palm leaves and tell him that his boss can dock advisor fees from my bill. That makes his face go all blank and confused again, so I shove at his arm and tell him the first one's on the house, but that doesn't seem to cheer him up as easily. Maybe I'm treating him more like the owner than a worker. I let the silence linger between us, hoping that maybe he will share. There are yards of opportunity, but instead of talking more, he drags me back into the arcade for a car race, which I win. Three times. He unravels back into the Nico I enjoy the most, as we play and I keep conversation to smack talk and weather and Simona Island.

Dinnertime sneaks up, and we share another meal together, talking about the sad state of French cuisine in North Carolina and how much Nico misses an American hamburger with bacon and cheddar.

Wandering the shoreline, shoes in hand, our conversation easily flows to the first time we saw the ocean and how life-altering it was. It's dark, and my shoulder bumps against his bicep with each step. His fingers nudge mine, then takes them, and with all the times he's touched me and led me somewhere, there's a difference. We slow, and his thumb trails over my knuckles with simmering warmth. Except then we spot Ruth walking toward us with an older gentleman, and before I can yell a greeting, Nico's back to frantically herding me toward the nightclub. But that's wonderful too, because we have a nightcap with Phil and Linda while Walt and Jose dance for us. Contrary to Walt's parodies, his man can move. They're beautiful together as they whirl, grins focused on each other. How lucky to be in love with a partner who fits you so well, you can both work and live together.

Walt heads behind the blue-lit bar to make another round of icy pink hurricane drinks, and after a hefty round of poke-fun-at-Cozette-for-not-knowing-there-was-a-real-hurricane, Jose steals me away to teach me to tango. Despite prompting, Nico stays put, watching with quirked lips until Jose's lesson gets downright obscene. While we grind to a Latin beat, Jose leans me back, running his fingers up my neck. He loudly threatens to steal me forever and break everyone's hearts. Walt warns him that Ruth is waiting to take his place as Walt's steady, but then Nico gets up, swings me into him, and shows us he actually can dance. A little.

"I'm out of practice," he says, spinning me the wrong direction and randomly dipping me off beat until I'm cackling while Jose coaches him from the sidelines.

When I yawn at ten-thirty, Nico drags me toward the hall and waves goodnight to everyone. We walk to the elevator, and I avoid a new mistletoe trap by flattening myself to the wall, scooching sideways like a sneaky ninja until we're past the kissy zone.

Nico avoids it with an easy sidestep and stalks down the middle of the hall. "You wouldn't take it seriously anyway."

My jaw drops as he pushes the elevator button. "I didn't Christmas curse and scan for an escape route, unlike a certain rule follower."

"I will own that I was...reluctant to publicly fraternize with a guest."

"Oh yeah?" We step inside the mirrored box like we're heading the same direction. "I had to kiss you because you froze and denying the tradition of mistletoe is bad luck."

"It is not." He pushes the five, and my insides tingle with nervous energy. "And I didn't freeze."

I blink at him. "Were you and I not in the same room? You were the non-magic version of Frosty." Making a Nico-in-headlights face, I stay perfectly still.

He pinches my side, making me squeak. "I needed a moment to think. But then you kissed me like I was your brother. It didn't count."

"It did too. The mistletoe gods are satiated." I fight my smile because I enjoy where this banter is going. "And I don't have a brother."

We step from the elevator and head toward my room, each step a question and a responding answer or doubt. Do I want this? *So much.* Am I ready? *Maybe.* What would James think? *It doesn't matter anymore, stop thinking about him.* Why am I thinking about him? *Because you broke up days ago.* It was over before then though. And Nico. *But secrets.* I can be patient. *But four days.*

"I don't think the mistletoe gods would approve of the platonic kiss you gave me," Nico says and hopscotches on the patterned carpet.

I follow his lead until we're at the door, where I can't stop myself from patting his chest, which turns into palming and moving closer. "It fulfilled its purpose. Plus, the blaring fraternization alarm spooked me." Sticking a finger against my ear, I wince. "That bitch is loud."

"It could have been louder." He inches forward all the way into the cutout alcove surrounding my door and slides a hand over my hip.

His biceps are firm under my fingertips, and I bite my lip. "Really? It was raucous."

"No, Cozi," he says, gaze adhered to mine and so close I notice the slightest ring of green around his pupil. He really does have ocean-colored eyes. "It would have sounded like this if it were really going off."

His lips press to mine, and heat blazes from his soft touch, then outright smolders when he dives in, parting me to him. A whimpery moan escapes as he seriously kisses me, firm and thorough and more intoxicating than any rum punch. Fingers dig into my back, and I arch against him, looping my arm around his neck and testing the silkiness of his hair with my fingers.

Wee-oo wee-oo. There is nothing familial about this kiss. Tingling need tightens my most fun places, and my breath quickens. We cling to each other, dancing with lips that follow the rhythm of rapid breaths and pulse, the gentle tap of teeth, the unfettered moans and responding husky hums.

"What changed your mind?" I pant as he tilts my head and kisses my neck.

"Needed more," he whispers and pulls me into a tight hug while his lips find mine again.

Too soon he slows and pulls away.

I need more too. "Do you want to—"

He quiets me with another deep kiss, then strokes my cheek and inhales under my ear. "I'll see you in the morning. Maybe at sunrise, if it's not raining."

I could tell him he can catch the sunrise from my room, or that he should stick around and see if Santa stops by, but the questions catch back up to us and I'm not sure I'm ready. It should be easy to hop into bed with someone and remember how I respond to new people again. Hell, I offered it to him already, but something holds me back. I want him, but there's something really beautiful in the want, and if—when that goes away, what will I be left with?

A few more days, then reality.

I nod, put in my code, and open the door, then drag him to me with a hand around his neck and give him another needy kiss.

As I pull away, he pecks me back and we end up stuck between room and hall, teasing tiny kisses out of each other. Finally, we both part and step away from each other.

"Goodnight," I whisper.

"Goodnight," he responds, looking back at me with half-lidded eyes and puffy, smirking lips as he walks down the hall.

The door clicks closed, and I blow out a long breath. O Christmas tree, am I in trouble with this one.

I pull my phone out and text Ilaria. She was still in the bar when we left, and I have a few things a concierge can help me with.

11

STORMY SNOW GLOBE

A fluffy pillow makes a decent shield against the intrusive alarm. Then my morning mind remembers why it's going off. I hop out of bed like a kid on Christmas morning, because *it is* Christmas morning.

I'm not a kid though. I'm very much a woman and planning to meet a handsome man for a sunrise cup of coffee. The view beyond the windows is darker than yesterday, and the palm trees are in constant motion, but there's no rain yet.

Texting my parents a long, rhyming Christmas message, I start the mini-coffeepot, then head to the shower. Ugh, it's so early.

The brain fuzzies scatter under the water. I've functioned on less than four hours of sleep before, and I'm out of practice, but it's Christmas. I have no family to hang out with, so I can nap the day away after I mess with Nico. Will he enjoy the scavenger hunt Ilaria helped me set up last night, or think it's childish? I only expected her to tell me where to find a few things for Nico even though it was late. But as usual, she went above and beyond, meeting up with me and even getting her daughter involved.

Xiamara works in the spa and is a certified aromachologist. Her profession took me several attempts to pronounce, and that was sober. She's adorable. A twenty-four-year-old version of her mother, with silky, shoulder-length curls, sparkling eyes, and an overly helpful but competitive personality. After making me sniff a concoction of essential oils she created to stimulate the prefrontal cortex of the brain to ignite focus and working memory, she handed over a pouch of good-sized charcoal chunks the spa uses to make their own mineral baths and masks.

After that she joined us on our hotel journey, patrolling for Nico sightings and pitching ideas of fastest or longest routes to make the game more challenging. She and Ilaria talked about training for this year's Moss Monster Meet, which Xiamara has won the past two years. The event sounds like a blast, with service-related challenges like the drink tray beach dash, the lost tourist jungle hunt, and the waterfall wedding ring retrieval. Of course, my mind exploded with ideas, but I stayed quiet and focused on hint hiding spots. Not my place.

When talk of the hurricane came up, Xiamara pulled a vial from her pocket and smelled a lemon-lavender blend she'd named Soothe Me Softly, then made me do the same to calm my amygdala. I was indeed soothed. Ilaria closed her eyes and took a long inhale as well, even though she's more concerned for the wildlife and landscaping. Cleanup after a storm is never a good time.

Sneaking around the hotel for two hours, we left a path of ten poetic Christmas clues around the hotel for Nico, with the last clue pointing to a bag of coal. Will he think it's silly or even get to run through it? He may be too busy prepping for the storm.

Maybe I can help with that. Or not, because I'm on vacation. If I get too antsy, I'll dive into my upcoming projects and see if there are any requests for event assistance. Maybe I'll luck out and someone will be looking for a small-scale training and team-building workshop at a tropical location that has good Wi-Fi. I have the perfect place.

I half-dry my hair, rushing when I peek out at the stormy morning sky. No Nico yet, but more people are out this morning. It's busy. Workers pin tarps over flower beds with sandbags and tie trees with rubber loops attached to other trees. Only a few of the lounge chairs remain, and they're taken by thrill-seeking early risers.

One thing I'm glad made it into my bag was my Christmas-patterned leggings. There are stripes of trees, candy canes, Santas, and reindeer over every inch. I pair them with a loose red tank top over a sports bra and put on my Santa hat. Best holiday outfit ever.

A coffee mug warming my hand completes my outfit, and I head down to say hello. Will Nico kiss me again today, or are we pretending last night's mischief didn't happen? He said he needed more, but then he got it and left, so maybe that concluded our fraternization law-breaking. I hope not. Another thorough kiss under the mistletoe with a beachy, coconut-and-vanilla-scented man is on my wish list this holiday.

On the patio, a gust makes me sidestep and pause, watching dark ocean waters crash in a raucous fight, as if each wave is vying for its own space and warning the other waves to back off. I pull my hat down lower. It's not cold, but the air is angry, pressing against me with a different type of chill.

Not quite a peaceful Christmas morning.

I feel my hair tug and I whip around to Nico's sweet smile. His beachy waves peek out under his own Santa hat. He's wearing a red, long-sleeve T-shirt and black trunks.

"Glædelig jul, Cozi," he says. "Merry Christmas."

Every time he speaks Danish, it's like he gives a teeny bit more of himself to me. I beam at him. "Merry Christmas."

He takes my hand and leads me over to the tethered trees,

cueing me to step over the cords. Leaning against the same one as yesterday, he sips his coffee and eyes me. "How are you this morning?"

Ah, fruitcake. We're going to ignore those delightful kisses. "I'm great. Feeling…festive." If I were home, I'd be in pajamas, sipping coffee and increasing the volume on the Christmas music as I wait for everyone to wake up so we could get this holiday started. I keep my disappointed gaze on the ocean and sip my coffee.

Nico snags my shirt and tugs, pulling me toward him until I'm facing the ocean and leaning back against a warm wall of handsome. "I like these pants," he says against my ear, letting his hand drift to squeeze my ass. Holiday hijinks are back on. Ho ho hell yeah.

"Me too. Unfortunately, it was too warm for my light-up Christmas sweater."

"This works," he whispers, then traces his lips over my ear. "You sure you're not cold?"

I'm certainly shivering. I bite my lip and drop my head back against his shoulder, keeping my hands wrapped around my mug. "Maybe a little."

He wraps his arm around me, sending the nerves on my hip into a riot under his teasing touch. There's no better way to enjoy the sunrise.

The sky is a different type of dramatic than yesterday, and there's not a single peep, caw, chirp, or buzz that makes the constant background song I didn't realize was the norm until the silence of this morning. Everything is ominous except for the peaceful bubble Nico houses me in.

Fiery orange pokes through tiny patches in angry clouds, as though attempting to get some stage time, but the clouds shuffle and block. Diffused light comes through the barrier as Nico traces his lips up my neck. He drops a line of gentle kisses.

The sunrise may as well be inside me, because I'm warm, bright, and ready to explode into a new day.

He works his way up my jaw and chin, then finally gives me the softest kiss I've ever had. Not the toe-curling scramble from last night, but a lazy morning greeting. *Hello, lips. It's wake-up time.* He traces more almost-kisses that tease the anticipation to a tight, needy tug between us. Eye to eye, breath to breath, who will pounce first?

"Breakfast," he whispers, inching back.

I refrain from whining, but it crosses my mind. Dropping my coffee cup to one hand, I turn to press as much of myself against him as I can and nuzzle against his vanilla-and-coconut-scented neck. "I'm good here, thanks."

I'll live in this moment as long as possible, frozen in a snow globe of a windy beach scene with roped-up trees.

He skims his fingers over my lower back, sending my skin into melty madness.

"No snorkeling today," I sigh.

"No."

I peek up at him, keeping my head on his shoulder. "What are we going to do?" I blink, knowing the exact type of mischief we can get ourselves into.

The corners of his lips turn up. "Oh, there are all kinds of things we can do today."

"Really?" I hold my breath.

"Yeah." He dips so close, the electricity of his proximity sparks against my lips. "Let's start with breakfast."

He pushes off the tree, taking me with him and dragging me toward the hotel.

"You're a tease," I tell him, trailing behind him. "Straight up naughty."

He turns with a smile, walking backward. "Then I'm in good company."

Breakfast is incredible. Holiday-themed pastries lay among

savory dishes surrounded by garlands, shells, and ornaments. In the middle of one table, they've stacked sliced fruit in the shape of a Christmas tree. I take pictures and send them to my parents.

As Nico and I are finishing peppermint coffee and discussing how one client wanted me to use a live elephant as a centerpiece for their circus-themed twenty-first birthday—I made them settle for an ice sculpture with multiple liquor luge ramps—my parents send a picture. They have matching Santa sweaters and stand next to a huge Christmas tree. Their plates hold sausage, what looks like latkes, and tree-shaped puff pastries.

"Aw," I coo.

"Your parents?" Nico asks quietly.

Guilt shoves away all happiness over my adorable parents. Nico doesn't have family anymore. Did he have happy holidays when he was a young kid? Not my place to know unless he wants to share.

I hand my phone over to him. "Yes. Introducing Bernard and Bernadette Fay, and no, I'm not making that up."

"That's adorable, actually."

"Oh, it is. When I was little and got in big trouble, they'd threaten to change my name to Bernadine if I didn't behave. That was my ultimate nightmare and more effective than any time-out."

"I can't imagine you as anything other than Cozette." He studies the picture. "Where is this?"

"Quebec."

His scrunched-nose expression makes me laugh, and I stand. "I know, right?"

"Not this time of year. Send them one of the beach." He hands me back my phone and takes my hand.

We head out to the patio, and I hold my phone up to take a selfie with the crashing waves behind me. It doesn't feel right. I tug Nico's hand. He steps close, although with a moment of hesitation, then takes my phone. "I have longer arms."

He bends and snaps a picture of us smiling, and I send it to my parents. That gets me a phone call in three seconds.

Nico laughs. "I have to check a couple of things this morning, but there's Christmas cookie decorating and Ilaria keeps mentioning Christmas caroling. You in?"

"Yeah. I'll be swinging in the breeze for a few." I point to the one hammock left assembled. The sky may be ominous, but it's not raining or too chilly. I haven't been in a hammock in a decade.

Nico runs his knuckles over his chin as I answer the phone. He takes that moment to take my hand and kiss it, not all that different from how he kissed me last night, and I nearly buckle to the tile. I give him a bring-those-lips-back glare, but he nips the pads of my fingertips and retreats, grinning before stepping inside.

"So," Dad states in his firm tell-me-everything tone. "Who's the tropical Santa Claus?"

Eyes flicking back to the building, I walk toward the trees and run my fingers over soft blue fabric. "Hang on, I have to tackle this phone call hammock-style."

"Oh ho ho—" He lets that last "ho" go long as I put the phone in my pocket and maneuver myself into the peapod-shaped cocoon.

I wiggle into place, core muscles tense as I try not to fall out. Once I relax, I pull out my phone. "Merry Christmas to you too. That's Nico. He..." Silver bells, I can't tell them much. "He works here."

"Mm-hmm," Dad mumbles.

"Put her on speaker," Mom says in the background. There's a mumble and shuffling noise. "He's handsome," she says, with the echo of speakerphone-land.

"He is." He's a great kisser too. And he makes me laugh and

feel an array of emotions I haven't felt in a while, even though I was in a relationship.

We catch up on our vacations, with most of the conversation veering back to Nico, making me have to reshift topics to keep from lying, then having to shift again when Mom brings up James—not sounding sad like I thought she would, but instead wondering if he was in New York or with his parents. I blurt out that he's working, then a bunch of stuff about empanadas and meeting Jules. We end our call with Dad telling me to watch out for couches, and I'm glad I finished my coffee or I would have choked. Apparently, we're adding pornos-on-couches jokes to our repertoire. I will have to prepare.

The strong breeze shifts the hammock, but not enough. I drape a leg over the edge and kick my foot to rock. The palm leaves rasp against each other in a rhythm that makes my eyes droop and flutter open and closed.

The hammock shifts, and my eyes pop wide to Nico, gracefully sliding in beside me.

"Go back to sleep," he whispers and tucks me under his arm.

I close my eyes and nuzzle against his neck. "You weren't gone long, and you're missing your Santa hat."

"Ilaria stole it and kicked me out. Prep is done."

He strokes my arm and plays with my hair. Relaxing against his warmth, I drift.

The sound of palm leaves whipping together wakes me. The wind has picked up. I study Nico's sleeping profile through the after-haze of my tropical winter's nap. Up close, he has a faint line of freckles across his cheeks and the most perfect nose—straight and sized exactly right for his face. I lightly ski my finger over the slight slope.

He turns his head to face me. Today, his eyes are bluer than the ocean. The wind sends his hair in a whirlwind.

"Have you talked to James?" he asks.

A cold chill replaces my fuzzy warmth. "Not since Sunday."

"After rum punch night?"

I nod, watching my fingers as I rub circles on his chest.

"Are you going back to New York after you leave here?" His voice lacks the playfulness I've grown accustomed to in our few days together. Maybe I am more than a passing guest.

"No." I bring my eyes to his. "Well, yes, I have to get my stuff out of the apartment, but then...I'm not sure yet, but James and I are officially done."

Sliding his fingers against the base of my skull, he pulls me into a hard kiss. I palm his chest, readying to give him a gentle push. We're in a hammock in a public location and this is... newlywed worthy. Sure, I'm glad he's tossed that fraternization thing out of the sleigh, but there's no need to throw it in the elves' faces. He's the owner. I'm a guest and—

My thoughts go to the wayside with the slide of his tongue against mine and his fingers tightening in my hair. His desperation is contagious. A fat drop of water hits my cheek.

I ignore it, but Nico pulls from me and looks up at the sky.

"Oh, hell," he says. "Let's go." The impossible way he hops out of the hammock makes me wonder if he sleeps in one at night. He drags me up. "Run for it."

"What?"

"Go inside." He untethers the hammock with two agile clicks, slings it over his shoulder, and shoos me toward the hotel.

Drip, drop, whoosh. The sky opens in a torrent of rain. I squeal and duck my head as if I can escape the barrage of water as we dash over the sand. We leap up the patio, and Nico jerks the door open for me.

"Such a gentleman," I yell over the rat-a-tat of raindrops.

He shuts us in, and the sound softens to a whispered pitter-pat.

"That is enthusiastic rain." I hold my drenched shirt out to keep it from sticking to me, while water drips from the white puff on my Santa hat.

"Welcome to the tropics. Our rain is indeed enthusiastic." The darkening sky is threatening past the glass. "It's starting?"

"It is." Nico shifts the wet hammock to hold in front of him. His shirt is dry where it had been over his shoulder. "We can get changed and then lunch?"

"I'm stuffed from breakfast." I peek in the dining hall as we pass. There's a huge group of people milling about tables set up beside the Christmas tree.

"Christmas cookie decorating," Nico says, answering my unasked question. "I'll meet you there." He kisses my cheek and heads down a hallway next to the dining room.

Aw. He liked my idea.

I snap a picture of my soaked self and text it to my parents. *Took a nap in a hammock while the storm rolled in.*

With Nico? My mom texts back, also sending a picture of the snow-covered Dickens village streets.

I ignore the question and head upstairs to change out of my drenched clothes.

12

SAUCY GINGERBREAD

"Hello, my beautiful American flower!" Jose yells from the lobby, scaring the Krampus out of me.

I stumble and pivot to wave at him and Walt, who's leaning over the welcome desk talking to Jennifer. "Merry Christmas, lovies. How was your Christmas Eve?" I glance back toward the dining hall, but Nico's not waiting so I head toward the men.

"Slow after the dance show," Jose says with a pouty lip as they meet me halfway. "Where's your delectable sidekick?"

I tilt my head, and Walt gives a mischievous chuckle, slapping Jose's chest with the back of his hand. "Shall we attempt to maintain an iota of professionalism, my love? Cozette doesn't work here."

"She will when I seduce her and keep her forever." Jose waggles his dark brows at Walt's glare and steps forward to bring me to him, stepping into a tango. "When this thing passes on, we should show you around the island. There's a waterfall you would love to see."

"Would I?" I ask as he spins me.

"It's a beautiful island, full of heavenly little spots to explore. I've been here five years, so I know all the best spots."

"Did you move here together?" I ask, whirling by Walt.

"Nope," Jose answers. "My Casanova arrived from Virginia a year ago."

"Almost two," Walt adds.

"Did you know each other before that?" They're the kind of couple who seem like they've been together forever.

They both laugh, showing all teeth.

"Oh no," Jose says. "Walt avoided me when he arrived. Can you believe it? He took his time warming up to me."

Walt crosses his arms. "I was new, and you were overwhelming."

"Gasp!" Jose says. "Moi? I haven't a clue what you're talking about." He dips me with flourish, then sends us into a centrifugal force-driven twirl.

I laugh. "Dance me in that direction, charmer. I have to meet Nico." I point down the hall—or try to, as we're spinning fast.

He abruptly halts. "Oh yeah?"

"Jose," Walt warns a half-second before Jose yells "Yes!" so loud, half the Caribbean probably heard him. "I mean. Yay." He shakes his fist in the air. "You're here until Friday?"

I nod, already feeling a chill cloud over the warmth of being included. I do want to explore this island. I want to see a waterfall, find little secret spots, and attend unique events. There are hints of a culture I haven't dove into yet scattered around the hotel and in the breezy attitudes of the people. I'm not going to have time to experience it all, especially during a storm.

Jose snaps me closer and foxtrots toward the dining hall. "We must enjoy every second with you that we can. Where are we going?"

I straighten my posture and follow his lead. "Dining hall, please."

"Cookies," Walt groans with his tongue lolling out. "K, let's go. Cookies." He speeds off, arms punching out and hips wiggling.

The buzz of laughter is raucous over instrumental Christmas music as we dance into the dining hall. Nico's not here yet, but Ilaria flits around a double table setup as six couples, a few of them familiar, and a staff member hunch over cookies, bags of colored icing, and bowls of edible embellishments. A few other guests mill about, munching on handheld pastries and sipping what looks like eggnog from blue glass goblets.

Jose twirls me away from him, letting go, and I step up to the table, eyeing the spread of decorated cookies. This innocent holiday event has taken a turn. Jose and Walt guffaw at the other side of the table, arms linked as they slowly walk and scan the creations.

"Cozi!" Linda bounces in her chair at the head of the table. "Cozi, look!"

Her cheeks and nose are pink from imbibing, and she holds up two decorated cookies, pressing them together. They're glitter-sprinkle boobs, and one has a blue-icing nipple ring. She makes them dance through the air, and I cover my mouth with my palm as laughter at her excitement bursts from my chest. "Those are glorious, Linda."

She places them in front of her own chest and shimmies. "Woo, woo, woo."

Phil chuckles and takes the goblet from in front of her, downing the remainder of its contents. "Should we get you one of those little rings, wild woman?"

Linda gasps and puts down her cookies to smack her husband's shoulder. They're so sweet. The colorful, decorated holiday shapes range from pure Christmas sweetness to downright naughty. The gingerbread men received the brunt of adult humor.

I point to one in bondage gear. "Nice use of licorice rope."

"Gracias," an older man says with a wide grin. The woman beside him releases a fury of giggles and fans her red face.

Ilaria tugs me to an open chair, leaning to talk. "Have you given him his present yet?"

"No," I whisper. "I fell asleep in a hammock instead."

"We saw."

My eyes widen. "Who's we?"

Maybe I was right to consider pushing Nico away, even though that attempt lasted a whole sixteenth of a second until he blasted my senses apart with his kiss. She flicks her eyebrows and pushes me into the chair. Walt and Jose eye me with matching know-it-all grins before dropping beside Phil and Linda to chat.

"Good afternoon," Peter says, passing me a full goblet.

It has cinnamon sprinkled on top and smells a little like Nico. I fall in love with a sip of the creamy coconut and rum concoction.

"Coquito," Ilaria mentions, like I should know the word, then wanders to talk to a lesbian couple about their perfect, vibrant cookies as Peter places a few small trays covered in green pouches on the table.

"Eee!" Linda squeals. "Pasteles. These are sooo good." This paradise has done Linda and Phil well. They are lighter than the day I met them in the van, dropping age with each day of sun and incredible food and every night of drinks, dancing, and whatever those longing looks they give each other lead to.

The guys stand, hands full of cookies, and wander back to me, planting kisses on my cheeks. "Come see us tonight, my American flower," Jose says. "Bring Nico along. We so enjoy the two of you."

The two of us, huh? I bite at my untamable smile.

With Walt's nudging, they wander out the door. Others pass over blank cookies and sugar supplies, and I get to work, taking delicious sips in between.

"Nice script," Nico says, pulling up a chair beside me. He holds a plate in his palm and takes a bite. "Mmm. Taste this." He holds out a forkful.

It's mouthwatering braised pork, I think, and it's perfection. "Were I Santa, that's what I would ask people to leave out instead of cookies." I'm tempted to tell him that Jose has requested our presence tonight, but I don't want to mess with the comfortable air around us by tossing coupley things at him.

"Pernil asado? Roasted pork?" Nico asks. "Instead of these..." He signals to the table, then tilts his head. His eyes go wide. "Oh."

"Yes, and maybe some sweet potatoes." I take a picture of my glitter cookie that says, *Ho Ho Hot Stuff*.

"I don't have sweet potatoes." He gives me another bite, sending me into a happy hum. "Is that a ball gag?" He eyes the table of goodies with a furrowed brow and points with the fork.

I find where he's looking. "Aw, a match to the roped-up gingerbread man. That's one big nonpareil." The pearly ball sits between red icing lips.

"Nothing phases you, does it?" Nico asks.

I tut at him. "I'm an event planner. I've seen it all."

His fork scoops the last bite, and he offers it to me.

I grin and accept the offering. "Thank you." I would rather have kissed him as a thanks, but this is all...new. As I stand, the dining chair legs hop over the low-pile carpet. "I have a present for you."

"Oh yeah?" He raises an eyebrow, and his eyes trail from my flip-flops up to the damp bun on my head. His lips part and he wets the bottom one, tongue peeking out, then sweeping it under his teeth.

A jolt of heat floods between my legs and tightens everything below my holiday sweater. I shift with discomfort. *Whoa.* When was the last time a lust-filled look made me squirm? The realization that it was before James is comforting—I'm not with him anymore. I've made the right decision. The part that sets me on edge is that I'm leaving in a couple of days, and the man that makes my insides quake lives here.

Ilaria snatches Nico's empty plate and he stands. "Are you okay?"

Nope. Not at all. "Yes." I swallow hard and pull the first clue from my shorts pocket. "Here."

Ilaria dances behind Nico as he reads.

His head jerks up, and his eyes sparkle with joy and mischief. The tightness in my nether regions takes a quick journey up to warm my heart.

I am so snowed.

13

GIVE ME A HINT

I follow Nico down the hall on the second level—well, I chase him, because he's fast when he's excited.

Apparently, treasure hunts excite him.

He mumbles the ninth clue in my ten-clue hunt again. "The next place to dash does this like the bells on Blitzen's sash. Like. Like, like...bells, sells, shells..." He halts and glances back at me. "Shells? No wait, what would shells have to do with bells beside rhyme? Dwell? What dwells with bells? Ribbon, reins, leather, um."

I bite my grinning lip. Nico thinks out loud, and his process is a creative sprint through wide options as he checks off illogical matches. He's quick, and I'm glad I went with harder clues. This little game would be over if I'd gone with simpler stocking hunt versions.

"Maybe..." he says, squinting one eye as he thinks. "Okay."

He dashes by me, dragging me along. Pausing in the stairwell, he glances up, and raises an eyebrow. I bite my lips. The first few clues could have been interpreted to lead to my room, and that was the first place he dragged me, before sighing when he realized I'm very serious about my scavenger hunts. Not finishing because we got caught up in a couch situation was unacceptable. He reads each new clue with his hand on my hip or his knuckles skimming my arm or his fingers stroking mine. Once an idea comes to him, he dashes off, leaving me with a great view. I'm anxious to see that muscular backside without the cover of swim trunks, and I nearly regret not ending the hunt with a lead to my bedroom. A hint like that would be too obvious though. How many women have led him to their bedrooms? I don't want to be like the others. Am I? I don't think so. I'm nothing like his ex.

I focus on how his hand engulfs mine, locking me to him as we head down to the lobby, where a long sash of ribbon decorates the front desk. Rain pelts the first set of doors. Beyond the drenched glass, short shrubs and trees whip and bend together in a wicked dance. The calm inside is quieter than usual, or seems that way because of the torment outside.

Nico pops up from his failed ribbon examination and glares back at me. "You're not even going to give me a hint?"

"Nope."

He glances up, and my eyes follow to see I'm stationed right under the mistletoe.

Nico crosses to me in three fast steps, grabs my face in both his warm hands, and gives me a kiss that heats me like I chugged a mug of too-hot cocoa.

"Huhm," I moan when he abruptly releases me, and my cheeks heat when I catch a wide-eyed, knowing smile from Jennifer.

"Rings! Bells ring like..." He dashes behind the desk, dodges her, and fumbles around. "The phone rings. Ah ha!" He holds up the final clue.

He reads in silence as he walks toward me and rests a hand on my hip. His eyes flick back to the beginning of the sentence again, then he smirks. That was fast, which was by design. While the middle hints can create frustration and take time, the last should be a near giveaway that leads to the present on a positive, excited high.

Ilaria and Xiamara helped me with this one.

If Santa had time to stay, he would head here for supplies to play.

The basement storage area is a stockpile zone of activity and event supplies. I could live down there for a week cataloging and creating an activity plan based around that goldmine.

Nico takes my hand and walks the hallway the staff often takes. We travel a narrow stairwell. It's unpainted concrete but clean and lit with a line of windows on each level. The door at the bottom leads to a lower, short hallway. Is his room down here somewhere, tucked away like a secret bunker? There are doors the ladies and I didn't go in or talk about last night. Nico speeds up as we pass into the storage area.

I pause in the middle of the room as Nico circles, taking in the parasailing and scuba gear, umbrellas, and hiking poles. Four kayaks are stacked on a floor-to-ceiling mount on the wall farthest from the door. I try to keep my eyes to myself to not lead him over to the second one. He passes under six bicycles hanging from a ceiling mount. Peeking at me over his shoulder, he throws open a gray metal storage cabinet containing an organized mess of event odds and ends. Half a pink feather boa escapes its shelf.

He pulls his eyes off me to search. "I wouldn't even know what to look for in here."

I press my fingers to my lips to keep from laughing at his disgruntled mumbles as he moves plastic bins around, then tries to fit them back in the space other items have decided to occupy. The boa gives him the most trouble.

He finally closes the doors and glares at me. "It's not in there, is it?" I shrug as he stalks over and leans close, cheek skimming against mine. "Give me a hint?" he whispers, tickling my ear with his lips.

"What are you going to give me in return?" I say back, voice breathy. He's not touching me, but he's so close.

Fingers brushing my hip, he leans back, parting his lips to say something, but his eyes catch on the kayaks. His lips quirk. "Hold that thought."

He steps away, leaving me overheated and agitated. I didn't understand what it meant to ache for someone before, but that's what's happening. My bits are swollen and antsy. My sweater is no longer comfortable because my breasts long to be free for his perusal. And my shorts are a prison, though I don't think my leggings would have been better. My skin longs to be against all of his sexiness.

The red ribbon of his gag gift peeks out of the green kayak's cockpit, diverting my thoughts. A nervous flutter dances through my stomach. Maybe I should have left him the real present—not that it's impressive, but this was a long treasure hunt for a bag of charcoal. He may not think it's as funny as I do.

He makes a show of pacing in front of it, hand on his chin like he's considering what it could possibly be. When he peeks back at me, I mouth, "tease." One side of his lips perk up, and he reaches in. He examines the bag with furrowed brows, and I nibble on my thumb as he opens the pouch.

"Coal?" His eyes light up, and he clutches his stomach with his free hand. "I can't believe you!"

"I, uh, it's not your only present."

"You do think I'm naughty." He walks over, staring inside the bag, but when he gets to me, he lifts my chin and gives me another one of those gentle kisses. "That was so much fun. Thank you."

"I'm glad." I trail my fingers over his chest. "I enjoyed putting it together. More fun to watch you run through it."

We've gotten closer. His arm slides around my waist, and he walks me backward.

I follow like we're dancing. "Where are we headed?"

"Upstairs." He kisses my neck, then my chin and my lips. "I have something for you too."

"You do?"

His grin tempts me to kiss him back before he answers. His grip on me gets tighter, and we bump into a wall. My fingers find warm skin under his shirt. It's like the sun soaked into him and he's been storing it during the storm. He tilts his head, pressing me against the hard surface with a kiss that lives between desperation and impatience. The flicker he sparked earlier bursts into a blazing yule log.

"Nico," I whimper and wrap my leg over his hip, needing to rid myself of the ache he's caused.

The bag of coal thunks to the floor as his fingers glide over my thigh and under my shorts. "Cozi," he answers and grinds against me, hissing through his teeth.

Everything tingles. Needs. Wants.

A door shuts from down the hall, and two male voices converse in mumbles. Nico and I fly apart. I blow out a long breath and shift my clothes back into place.

Nico adjusts himself with a wince. "Um, yeah okay, we should go."

I snort and cover my mouth. When I was younger, I was too busy to be caught in the storage room with anyone, but I think it would have been like this. My heart is racing, my entire body is hot, and holding back giggles is next to impossible.

Grinning, Nico shakes his head, snatches the coal from the ground, and nudges me toward the hallway. We wave at the two men as they enter the room with armfuls of chairs. Their conversation halts.

"Inventory check for something to do indoors," Nico says, walking faster.

They nod and continue on, glancing back a couple of times as we dart toward the stairs.

Nico squeezes my hand. "How did you know about that place?"

"How do you think?" I debated whether to use the storage room because guests don't have all-access like I do.

His hand lands on the small of my back, and he turns the pouch of coal in his hand. "Ilaria."

"Yep." My body is not happy with the constant state of lust it's living in. Though it's not entirely his fault with the interruptions, he's teased me into a wobbly-legged, insides-trembling mess. I want his fingers everywhere, not only lightly guiding me around.

He seems like he wants to say more as he works his lip and we meander up the stairs, but silence remains until we step out in the upper hallway. "The treasure hunt was sweet, Cozette. I haven't had that much fun in a long time."

"Me either."

His nose crinkles. "I doubt that. You bring joy to everything you do."

"That's kind to say, but it's been a bit since I've been able to do anything like that. It wasn't appreciated, so I didn't try."

"That is a serious shame." He squeezes my hand, then releases it. "I have to go get your present. Shall I bring it to your room?" He tucks his lip under his teeth, and he better not be kidding with me.

I tug his lip free with my finger and grin. "Yes. Bring it up, please." I glance around like we're sneaking, then go up on tiptoes to give him a quick kiss. "See you in a few."

Fanning my face on the elevator, I take inventory. Nico likes me. He's dropped the secretive interest and affection. Even if it's temporary forbidden-guest lust. He makes things happen in my body that I haven't experienced in a long while, if ever. What present could he have gotten me? If he were James, it would be a planner or something practical. Nico doesn't seem practical though—or at least, he balances the practicality with fun.

If downstairs was any indication, we're probably going to have sex. There's still that pesky I-know-who-you-are thing poking at my brain, but this doesn't need to be serious. In a couple of days, I'll be gone and his secrets will remain his. We can call this the sexiest Christmas ever and remember it each year with a smile.

Easy peasy, elves are sneezy.

14

MISTLELOW

Trembling, I freshen up only a little. I leave my hair in the messy bun but brush my teeth and wash my hands. The rain smashes against the windows as I kick off my flip-flops and grab the real present I made him last night, running my thumb over the curly red ribbon.

The gift shop stays open late and has small, quirky bobble-head dolls. One looked somewhat similar to Nico, and with the starfish pendant I've glued to its face, it's close enough and still bobbles.

Each passing minute makes me shiftier. A bottle of water aids my dry mouth. I crush it when my phone buzzes and water squirts out of the top. "Snowflakes!" I wipe up the water and check my buzzing phone.

It's James. *Merry Christmas. I hope it's happy for you.*

Nope. I will not reply. All I'm filling this day with are tons of perfect kisses from a hot, tropical Santa who takes me on adventures like playing with sharks and getting sexy in a hurricane. Merry Christmas to me. Shoving my phone in my pocket, I drop backward over the arm of the couch, letting my feet flop over the edge. What if Nico changes his—

A knock on the door has me up so fast, the dim room swirls. I take a deep breath. The door opens, wafting in the scent of hallway and vanilla, shoving away any errant thoughts beside Nico's smiling lips and the brown box with a blue ribbon in his arms.

I eye the rectangle box. "It's big."

"Thank you," he says with a wide grin.

"Nico," I groan. "Get in here."

He sets the box on the kitchen counter and stares at the Christmas tree with the rearranged ornaments.

"Oh, I...uh, repositioned some ornaments."

"It's better that way." He keeps his eyes on the tree for another moment, then focuses on me.

I hand him my gift. "Should we open these together?"

He shakes his head. "Open yours. I want to watch."

I run my finger over the top of the box. "Is it a remote control car?"

"No. Do you want one of those?"

"Maybe. They're fun." The ribbon slips slowly apart with a tug. "Is it a puppy?"

"I'd take you to adopt a puppy if it were a puppy."

I blink at him. "You would?" Visions of throwing a ball on the beach for two rambunctious mutts has me wrapping my arms around Nico's neck.

"Yeah." He grabs my waist to keep me from pressing against him, and pink tints his upper cheeks. Maybe he struggles as much as I do when we touch. Or maybe bringing up dogs is too heavy a conversation. He spins me around but keeps a hand on my hip. "Open."

I flick the tape and flip up the box lid. It's a familiar and missed holiday necessity. "Bûche de Noël!" I say behind my hands. "Nico."

It's prettier than the ones I've made with my family each year and even has confection holly leaves and berries. There's a sign made of chocolate with block writing. *Veux Fraterniser Avec Toi.*

"I want to fraternize with you?" I ask between giggles. Tugging my phone out, I swipe away another message from James without reading it, take a picture of the cake, pull the sign off, and do it again. Explaining the present to my parents is going to be difficult enough without the personal message attached.

He runs his hand through his hair and shrugs a shoulder. "Sounded funnier last night."

"It's hilarious. I love it so much." I toss my phone in an empty drawer, then grab two forks and hand him one. "How did you know?"

"Rum punch night. You told me this would be the first year you didn't have one. I couldn't have that." He points to where I stashed my phone. "You okay?"

Am now. James can text the drawer all he wants. My mind is calm with my decision and— "I am very much okay. It's Christmas and I have bûche de Noël." And Nico. I turn to the cake and gather a forkful from the edge. This was seriously thoughtful. The dark chocolate is more decadent than I've ever had and is a blissful distraction from my thoughts. It's smooth, with a bitterness that mellows the sweet cake. "Rudolph's red nose, this is unbelievably good."

Nico chuckles and grabs a forkful. "Mmm, I did well then?"

"You did perfect." Too perfect. A step up from boyfriend perfect. I cup his cheek and kiss him, hoping that will dissipate the lump of emotion in my throat. "Did you make this?"

"I did...under the watchful eye of a French chef who doesn't get to bake as much authentic French as he should."

"Thank you. That was...I'm really appreciative." I take another bite and raise an eyebrow. "What did Jules say about your sign?"

"He didn't see the sign. This is superb. I've never had one."

I tilt my head. "How did you make it in French then?"

"I'm fluent in French."

He understood the conversation between Jules and me? He also knows Spanish, English, and Danish. "How many languages do you speak?"

He takes a bite and a long breath. Was that too personal? Maybe. I open my mouth to change the subject, but he answers, "Nine. Danish, Swedish, and Norwegian, but those are similar. German, Dutch, Mandarin—though not as well as I'd like—Spanish, French, and English." He kisses my parted still-in-shock lips. "It's a European thing. We pick up on other languages." He goes back to eating like it's no big deal to be able to say "cake" in nine languages.

I should stop gaping. I hand him his present. "Ouvert."

He grins. "Okay. Thank you."

"Don't thank me yet. You haven't seen it." My face heats.

He opens it with a laugh, then pulls the bobblehead from the box. "*Det er fedt.* This is the best present I've ever gotten."

I laugh. "Then you deserve way more presents, but I'm glad you like it."

He sets the starfish-face bobblehead on the counter, taps its head to send it wobbling, and cups my neck. "I love it. You are —" He blows out a long breath as his eyes wander my face. "You're something else." His playful expression drops to something more in line with my thoughts.

We surge together in a hard kiss. I moan into his mouth, and he fills his palms with my ass. No more interruptions. I want him and he wants me. I press close against him when something crunches between us.

Nico's cheeks were pink earlier, but now they've gone full sunrise. I pull back and take in his gray shirt. Nothing there, but lower…there's a bulge. Well, more than *that* bulge.

When I lift the hem of his shirt, I fail at attempting a

straight face. "There's a sprig of mistletoe caught up in your drawstrings, Nico." I blink up at him and nibble my lip.

His face is trapped in an embarrassed wince, and he rubs his forehead. "Um, yeah, I thought—"

I put him out of his misery with a kiss and slide down him to my knees. Eyes on his, I brush my lips over the fabric-hidden hardness, and he sucks in a sharp breath. My trembles subside with my new focus.

He wants a kiss below the mistletoe? I'm happy to oblige.

As I tease a line over his erection, he sucks his bottom lip and watches me. But when I slip fingers below his waistband to drag his shorts down his thighs, he grips my wrists and tugs me back up, kissing my pulse points.

"Cozi," he groans. It's a tone of agony that entices me to give him anything he wants. "I didn't expect you to—it was a joke...kinda."

Pressing against his chest, I nip his bottom lip. "You don't want me to suck your dick?"

"Oh, I do." His eyes crinkle at the corners with his grin, and his fingers twist in my hair to drag me forward, bringing us crashing together again. "But if it's okay with you..." he murmurs against my lips, free hand toying with the button on my pants as he walks me backward. "I want to be inside you. Nothing feels close enough when it comes to you."

Warmth unfurls like a blossoming hibiscus. "Yes, please."

15

MERRY AND RIGHT

I claw at Nico's shirt, tugging so hard I nearly take his head with it. We laugh, then he snaps to, jerking my sweater over my head and somehow slipping his hand under my unbuttoned shorts at the same time.

"Multitasker," I moan, as his warm fingers tease against silk and promise presents of skilled touch and laser-focused lust. I grip his hair and bite his ear.

He gives off the sexiest growl as he drags my bra strap down with his teeth.

I hum a breathless moan, impatient to learn every inch.

He flinches as my fingers lightly skim his ribs, and I jerk at the brush of his thumbs against my hips. We both give each other an apologetic grimace at the quick discovery of ticklish spots, then surge back together to explore more angles, more sounds, more ways to drive lust to a mountainous peak of stimulation. My body sings with it.

The area from the kitchen to the bedroom is an obstacle course we ping-pong through, attention strictly adhered to the frustrating remaining garments keeping us apart while we taste and touch each other. The Christmas tree jingles ornaments as we twirl by. My shorts hit the carpet and I nearly topple, but the arm of the couch and Nico keep me upright. He cups my ass and slides lower, massaging my inner thigh and so, so close to where I need him. I palm his biceps, grope his incredible shoulders.

"For a moment," he rasps, "I thought you may have the corset on under that sweater."

"Want me to put it on?" I ask as he explores my collarbone with his lips.

He groans. "Only if you don't mind it being in pieces. Do you have any idea how hard it was not to drag you into the van and rip that thing off you bit by bit?"

Aw, really? He was such a gentleman though. It's hard to believe that was only days ago. "Sounds hot," I say, kissing a path down his neck.

"You're hot."

I scoff. "Nice comeba—"

He lifts me, making me gasp, even though my legs naturally wrap around his hips. He stares up at me, one arm wrapping me securely against him. He traces my lower lip with his thumb, fingers stretching to caress the back of my neck and slowly drag me closer.

My mind scrambles with the heat of his gaze and the swell of need for him. This...we are definitely doing this. His smile is obvious between the kisses he places on me, prompting my grin as well, but then he presses me to the wall right outside the bedroom, guides my legs to standing, and teases the place that's tingling with cheer with his fingers. The ache is intense, I'm already halfway there, toeing the edge and writhing as I've never writhed before.

"*Du er så smuk.*" That had to be something sweet, with how his eyes wander me. He unsnaps my disheveled bra and tosses it over his shoulder. "So beautiful, Cozi." Tucking his face against my neck, his lips send a shiver through me as he moves down my collarbone and keeps going. "This okay?"

"Yes," I whisper, fingers clenching in his waves as he gently sucks my nipple, sending pleasure on a joyride down, landing straight between my legs, which he uncovers by slipping his thumb under the thread of lace and ever so slowly tugs down until my panties tickle my ankles. "Yes, yes, yes," I add in case he didn't catch the first one. More than okay. Required, desired, so very inspired. I hope his day is clear tomorrow, because I need to memorize the way he alternates between tongue and teeth. My wobbly knees almost give and I sink back, letting the wall hold me upright.

"Hold these," he says, pulling condoms from the pocket of the shorts hanging off his hips. He shoves down the last item keeping us apart and steps out of them, then lifts me off the ground again. I wanted another moment to take in all of him because, whoa, Nico, but can't complain about the heat of his skin against mine.

"Two?" I cling to him, nipping his neck as he walks into the bedroom. My panties dangle from one foot, and since I like his style of discarding clothing, I kick them off, not caring where they land.

"For a start." He tosses me on the bed. It's a chilly contrast, and I shift to my elbows, wanting him close again when the wind whips so hard against the building, it moves. I'd forgotten the hurricane. Outside is a dark riot of nature. Rain thrashes the windows in chaotic fleeting plinks without holding a rhythm.

Nico crawls over me and turns my face to his with fingers on my chin. When our eyes meet, the blue closing in chases away the storm. His kiss steals my breath, nipping at me until I'm smiling and looping my leg over his hips, trying to drag him to me. He skims his fingers over mine as he takes the condoms and opens one.

I kiss his shoulder and sharp collarbone, then impatiently take the contraceptive and roll it on, because I can't not touch him everywhere. He's velvet heat over steel, and while I want to spend hours, days, infinity studying each inch of him, he's right. We're not nearly close enough. He stays still over me, fists dipping the mattress next to my shoulders. His eyes flutter closed when I reach the base of him. I push up to nip his ear, and his sharp exhale makes me want to do it again and again for that fun reaction.

His fingers skim my thigh, while his lips return to bewitching my nipples. He switches sides and twirls his tongue, sending an ache through my whole breast and stirring up delight in my core.

I moan, then glare. "You're teasing me." I dig my fingers into his shoulder when his teeth graze again. I may explode and moan a warning siren.

"I am," he says with a grin, sliding his fingers between my legs. "And you like it." He raises an eyebrow and nibbles that lip. "Slippery."

I nod, panting like I'm in a race. I'm chasing down a building release, so that makes sense. "Worked up. Need y—"

With a pained groan, he replaces his fingers with his cock, filling me with warmth and bliss. With him.

I clutch at his hard sides and exhale a long, loud sigh.

Still as stone, he kisses me and brushes his nose against mine. "Everything good?" he whispers, words tickling my wet lips.

He's exquisite, his hips pressed to mine, enough weight on me to be the best of hugs, especially with how he's brought his arms in tight, as if he needs all of him touching all of me. "Mm-hmm, so good."

We kiss in the stillness of breathing and rain patters, connected tight with slow rolling hips. Then I guess Nico realizes we fit, our bodies tested and finding a match, and he loops an arm under my hips. If I thought he could move well in the water or on treasure hunts, I was wrong. The bed is his ultimate terrain. I plant my heels in the mattress and match the pump of his graceful but unyielding thrusts. He grinds each time his hips press to mine, sinking deeper and building the tension between my legs with a vengeance.

I whimper against his tongue. "Nico." I tense, thighs shaking, and hum little squeaky gasps.

"Mmm, taking notes." He pulls out, making me bare my teeth, but quickly turns me to face the mattress, lifting my hips, then gets right back to his perfect rhythm. The angle is tighter and even more maddening, enhanced with his surrounding scent and the comfortable dimness that makes everything hazy and beautiful, highlighted from the light spilling in from the glow of the lit wreath above the bed.

I bite my lip to keep from screaming out and white-knuckle the cushy pillows.

Nico's hot palm caresses my spine, making me arch.

"Good too, yeah?" he murmurs against my ear.

I make an incoherent, giggling moan. I doubt there would be a bad position with Nico, but *good* doesn't touch this. First-rate maybe? Cosmic comes to mind.

He kisses the back of my neck and tugs my hair band out to release my bun. "There is nothing better than right now." Then, because he refuses to play fair, he whispers naughty things...*in French*. He tells me the sounds I make sets him ablaze. That I'm impossible to stay away from. How he can't resist touching me, and I blush all the way to my nipples.

Arching, I peek at him over my shoulder and try out some words of my own. I whisper that I'd rather look at his eyes than the ocean, and how his lips are pure, tempting sin. In a moan, I tell him I want his hands all over me.

Holding me tighter, chest thrumming against my back with rapid breaths, he tells me he could live between my thighs.

I turn my head to lick his lower lip and quip that there's a tongue tax.

Dirty talk is way better in French. Not that I've participated in a dirty talk conversation before.

"Oh, Cozi," he says, switching back to breathy English. He cups my cheek, meeting my eyes. His face is half in dim light and half in shadow, and he's so beautiful I can't stand it. "I'll make so many pre-payments, I'll be able to build a city."

We kiss each other's laugh, and Nico moves us with a passionate pace that makes me fumble my wit and clutch the soft sheets. He's magic. The hottest, sweetest, most fun present I could have asked for on a stormy Christmas Day.

Simple and desperate is all I can manage, as I'm wound up tight with excruciating pleasure. "Touch me, please." He hasn't stopped touching me, but I'm haywire now as the escalating wave inside builds to breaking point.

He rotates me to face him again and holds me tight, fingers splayed against my back, heart thudding against mine. A near-frown on his lips would look angry if not for the serious heat in his eyes. I wrap around him, and with gasps and increasing fervor, we crash together, come together like the tormented waves outside.

In the echoes of our hard breathing, paused only by softly placed kisses, a tear slides down my cheek. The rain now registers as background noise. There are too many endorphins dancing through my body to be afraid. Heartbeats slow, Nico shifts to rest his face against my neck but makes no move to separate from me. I'm so glad for this dimly lit, coconut-scented, hot, and slightly sweaty cuddle.

I map his shoulder blade with one hand and the curls at the nape of his neck with the other. "Merry Christmas, Nico."

Nico lifts his head and brushes his smiling lips over mine. "Merry Christmas, Cozi."

16

HURRICANE NICO

*L*ight wakes me, as does the warm hand rubbing my hip.

There is such a thing as too much festivity, though as with all major celebrations, I have no regrets. And now I have four favorite positions and a vagina that ran a marathon when it only trained for a 5K. So worth it.

Last night, after we basked in the afterglow of discovering how well our bodies play together, we got a quick bite of dinner, teased each other with heated glances and subtle touches, then nearly fucked in the elevator on the way back to my room. He bent me over the couch after we fell through the door.

Later we had more bûche de Noël and talked about storms while we sat on the bed, rain and wind bludgeoning the floor-to-ceiling windows.

Nico's first hurricane experience was three years ago, and it scared him. El Escape proved its stability, even though it had only been completed months earlier. His pride shone through. I didn't press for information before Simona Island, but after a pause of focusing on the storm, he told me that growing up in

Denmark was similar to North Carolina when it came to weather, though a few degrees cooler. I thought my heart would burst from my chest as he reminisced about Danish summers and building snowmen in February.

I didn't interrupt him for fear of breaking the enchantment of sharing, though I had to bite my tongue when he told me about picking strawberries and making cakes. There are several farms near my parents' house where you can pick your own berries, and we are people who like our cake. Maybe he could visit...if this weren't a vacation fling. Nico gave me no time for difficult thoughts, because as the taps of rain against the windows replaced his words, he slid me onto his lap, spread me wide, and fingered me while we watched nature rage. I'll never look at a tropical storm the same way again.

After his big share, conversation stayed sexy or holiday-related. Our New Year's celebrations are similar, but where I hug and kiss everyone, Danes jump off chairs. Something bothered him about that conversation, so I dragged him off to the shower and tasted him.

He tackled me under the Christmas tree as we made our way back to the kitchen for water and bûche de Noël. He claimed it was to pay off his tongue-tax deficit, which made me laugh until I realized that man could monopolize my body if we had more time. After, when he carried me to the kitchen because my lower half was confounded by multiple orgasms, he stood between my legs as I sat on the counter and shared bites of cake as he taught me dirty talk in Danish. My failed attempts made him laugh, but then he'd kiss me thoroughly when I pronounced words correctly, which wasn't often enough.

We are ridiculous.

He encourages every sexy thing I do, and when I shock him, his eyes flash with fire and something that makes my chest warm with comfort and pride. There's no judgment. No pushback. No scorn.

"How are you feeling?" he asks with a morning rasp.

I stretch and turn toward him. "Ouchie and incredibly happy about it." I've never felt more me than when surrounded by Nico.

He smiles and strokes my face. Under my palm, his hard chest is warm from being pressed against my back. Thunder rumbles outside, and rain washes the windows, reminding me of driving through a car wash.

"How long will this go on?" I ask.

He kisses my shoulder, hands wandering. "No more than a day."

My nipple tightens under his attention, and I arch into his palm. Lips land on my neck and then he's over me, wedging his hips between my thighs. His groan in my ears is a perfect carol.

I grin and sink my fingers into his hair. "You're relentless, Nico."

He freezes, then backs away. "Sorry. I—"

Whoa, what happened? "Wait. Come back." I shake my head and follow his retreat, crawling up to straddle him. "I enjoy your relentlessness. It makes me feel wanted. See?" I take his hand and put it between my legs, then dig my fingers into his shoulders at the pleasure his touch gives. "I want you too."

His expression isn't happy. His eyes wander my face, lips parted like I've baffled him to dumbstruck speechlessness. I probably looked the same as I laid under the tree, looking up at the symmetrical branches of the artificial fir as he kissed the sensation back into my thighs. Until that moment, I wasn't aware that bliss could be so tenacious.

He pulls his fingers from me, puffs his cheeks to blow a long breath out, then hugs me, tucking his nose under my ear. "I never expected *you*."

That makes me smile. "I didn't expect you either."

Drinking, the beach, and working through the holidays was on my list of to-dos to get me through my breakup. I haven't opened my computer, except to do that one thing I shouldn't have. I cling to him tightly, and he misinterprets my guilt for need, which is for the better.

It hurts a little when he enters me, and I inhale through my teeth.

"Want me to stop?" he whispers, lips to my ear.

"No." I grin. "All is merry and right."

That gets a chuckle and languid movement from Nico. He's careful with my body this morning, but the seriousness of his gaze and the reverent way he touches me sends more pangs of guilt through me. He balances on his elbows and stares down at me, stroking my face with his thumbs, working between my thighs in a rhythm that resounds in my heart. I run my hands over now-familiar muscles. My leg hooks over his hip, and I can't imagine not having felt how his body fits mine. "This is paradise, Nico."

He is paradise.

It's his business what he tells me, but as I stare up at him, I want to steal all the thoughts behind his eyes. I should enjoy this for what it is—a temporary escape—but I already want more time on a clock that slowly ticks toward our parting. There are thousands of men in the world that may fit me just as well...but dammit, I want this one.

I want, I want, I want.

Nutcrackers, I've fallen for Nico.

Despite the thoughts snowballing through me, Nico brings me to the edge of bliss and pushes me over, holding me securely as he follows. We cling to each other as if at any moment what we've found may get dragged away.

Yep, falling hard.

We're both quiet. Too quiet for us. He rolls to lie beside me and holds my hand. The rain patters in a slow, steady beat.

"Why did you change your mind on fraternizing?" I ask, eyes to the ceiling. He napped with me in a public hammock, fed me from his plate, and kissed me in the lobby yesterday. Did he just forget himself, or is there more to it?

His chest rises high and falls in my peripheral vision. "I—um. There is no fraternization policy."

That gets my eyebrows up, and I turn, propping my head in my hand.

He crinkles his nose. "I saw you and we talked for five seconds, and I knew you would be a problem for me. It was an excuse to stay away."

I run fingers over his chest. He's been through a rough time, and I could understand his reluctance, but he didn't want to give me a chance? "I thought it was because I'd just broken up with someone, but you didn't know that until way past the five-second point."

The room mimics the quiet of the almost-sunrise. The main event is coming, and I need to be patient and wait for the curtains to open.

"Cozette." He closes his eyes. "I own the hotel. It can cause problems with guests and staff. It causes problems with women." His eyes open, but squint as if it's this horrible thing to own a hotel.

I sigh and part my lips to tell him...something. *I know? It's fine? Well yeah, duh, but it doesn't matter?* As happy as I am that the information is out there, words aren't coming to me. "Okay."

He sits up so fast I jostle next to him and sit up too. "Did you know?"

I grimace at his hard, seeking stare. I'm sure "sorry" is all over my face. I give an apologetic wince-shrug. "Yes."

"When?"

Why does he look so pissed? He takes his secrets seriously.

"The day I arrived," I say and nibble my lip. "It doesn't matter to me. Are you mad?"

There's a pause to him, a stillness as my words sink in and I can't stop it, but I know by the shift of his muscle and the hurt in his eyes that this may be torrential.

"The first fucking day?" He rolls from the bed like it's on fire. "Why didn't you say something?"

I didn't expect him to be happy if he found out I knew, but he's furious. I don't like him this angry. It doesn't fit him.

"It's not something you want people to know, right?" I ask, trying to keep my voice calm. "I thought I'd wait for you to tell me. *If* you told me."

He snatches his clothes from the chair in the corner, kicks his legs into his pants, then jerks his shirt over his head.

I jump up and head to the dresser to grab a shirt, unable to be more exposed with whatever is happening here. "Hey, it's fine, Nico. I don't care."

He strides to the front door so fast I have to jog to keep up. He slams the door before I can get through. Shit, I can't flash my ass. I sprint to the dresser and hop into pants, then run out the door.

"Nico, wait." The elevator dings, and I barely dash in before it closes.

He won't look at me.

I face him but give him some distance and lean against the metal wall. "Where is this coming from? Talk to me, please."

He stays quiet as the floor numbers blink by. I'm drawn to him, needing to get close because that's what feels natural, but he moves away before I can touch his arm.

"Don't," he growls.

"Fine," I say and lean back against the mirrored wall. "I'm not sure what's happening here. Do you want me to have a problem with you owning the hotel? Can you explain this to me?" While I'm not the best angry person, I'm good at dealing with them.

"Go back to your room, Ms. Fay."

Ms. Fay? He spent a good part of the night inside my body, and I'm Ms. Fay now? "Oh, don't give me that guest treatment shit. Think about this, Nico."

"I am!" he yells, still not looking at me.

"Then explain it to me, dammit, because we were having a great morning and I don't know where this is coming from." When he still doesn't say anything, I step closer. "Tell me."

He slaps the stop button, and we pause our descent. "You were too perfect. I didn't see it like I usually do. Disregarded the signs, your own words, when I knew better because I..." He trails off, shaking his head.

"See what? Signs? I'm just—"

"On a job interview?"

What the hell? "No. What?"

"No?" He finally faces me, eyes narrow and painted with red vessels. "You're a world-renowned conference director who randomly dropped out of the majors of your industry around the time you picked up a doof—" His lips press tight together, and he growls. "A boyfriend, then took a piddly-shit job. Why?"

I blink at him, attempting to process his words. "World-renowned, huh? Picked up?"

He has the decency to purse his lips and stare at the wall. "You could have made a new company with your credentials and contacts. Was it James? Did he offer you something or have connections you needed?"

"The only thing I needed was a lighter load to find my sanity, and James was there for me for my exhaustion meltdown."

"A convenient opportunity." He shakes his head. "That makes sense. I'm sure New York would be demanding compared to a place like El Escape. Now he's gone, and you end up in the Caribbean at a luxury resort."

"Convenient?" Damn you, rum punch, and damn you, Nico, for being so incredibly wrong. "James was never 'an opportunity.' We dated because we liked each other, but our relationship had been failing for a long time. I moved with him knowing I probably shouldn't."

Nico huffs. "Because you needed him."

"No. Because I was compromising to make it work. That's what you do in a relationship. But I couldn't sacrifice who I was anymore. I ended up here because my first job, the one that broke me, provided a big enough reserve that I could afford my first non-work-related vacation to the Caribbean when I had nowhere else to go for Christmas. Then I met you, and you seemed to appreciate who I really am, but now?" I signal at him, his fuming anger, and his glare filled with mistrust. "What the hell is this, Nico?"

His hard expression softens. Maybe he's found the rational part of his brain. "The way you plant ideas is a skill. Everyone who has met you will not shut up about how I should hire you, and you show off how capable you are at every corner right when your company is going under. Did you mention that to Ilaria and Ruth, or keep it quiet? How many of the staff have you spoken to about needing more time here?"

"Wait." I grip his arm and he doesn't shrug me off. "My company is going under? Holy shit, Nico, where did you hear that?"

"You didn't know?" His expression is less questioning than his words.

"I would have remembered that." He has to be wrong. Wouldn't I find out something like that before a hotel owner in the Caribbean?

He smacks the button and we're off again. "You're beautiful, incredibly clever, impossibly charming, and overly successful for your age besides the hiccups in your career path—it fits."

"Thanks, I think. But it doesn't fit. I didn't even know I was headed to Simona Island until the day I arrived. My only goal was to have a fun holiday." I cross my arms as the elevator door slides open. "And then I was too busy in the land of flirting and multiple orgasms with the guy I like to consider pursuing a job I don't need."

Nico snorts and scoots by the wide-eyed couple waiting at elevator doors. I give them an apologetic wince and step after him.

"No matter how quiet I keep," he whispers. "It's not possible to be normal. That's what my public relations guy always tells me. *Everyone* wants something from me, Cozette."

"Not me. I don't care about your money or getting a job. I care about you."

"Sure you do." He rolls his eyes. "Others have said that too. Money changes everything. Being who I am changes everything. I should have kept traveling with a damned backpack, but I wanted to settle, and there's no better place than here. I can't escape the past, my wealth, and I'm too weak to walk away from it all. I was too weak to walk away from you. Then you...lie."

"I didn't lie." I wanted him to share, and here we are. Sharing up a storm. I grit my teeth to fight the ache behind my eyes. "I'm not the others." I try to jump in front of him, but he sidesteps and keeps on his path.

"No?" he asks, eyebrows up. "They kept quiet too. Pretended they didn't know or care. Then they'd ask if I still had connections to—" He shakes that thought off, whatever it was. "They'd tell me they were being evicted, or a private, highly exaggerated conversation would end up online. There would be a paternity accusation." He snorts, and his jaw flexes with tension. "Are you recounting last night to the tabloids?"

"What tabloids? The Simona Island Press?" My laugh is sharp and huffy. I bring my fingers up to slide through the air with my words. "Headline reads: *Local hotel owner makes French cake and gives great tongue.* Seriously? Oh, my god, Nico. I'm not your ex."

He jolts to a stop and glowers at me. "What do you know about her?"

Dammit. Everything's all flamey, and I just tossed on another yule log. This is what happens when people don't talk about things they should talk about. When I stay quiet, attempting to quell the fire, he storms off again down the hall, pauses, turns back to me with gritted teeth and finger in the air, then spins again and keeps on stomping. "Go."

He's more tumultuous than the tropical storm.

I follow him. He's mad, hurt, and has a barge-load of baggage, but I've gotten to know him over the last few days. This isn't him, and he's not seeing my side.

He shoves open a back door that puts us in a flooded parking lot where two vans are parked. Wind sets me off-balance before tapering off.

"Did she send you?" he asks, forging ahead.

I shake my head, even though he's not looking at me. "I would never speak to that woman or do what she did." Rain randomly smacks me in fat drops, and water splashes under my bare feet as I jog after Nico. I have to dodge a few palm branches. "I'm sorry I googled you, but I only saw headlines and one article. I didn't dive in, but I'm not the only one looking into others, am I?"

His fists clench at his sides.

"Don't be a hypocrite, Nico. You didn't search my name on the internet? See that I was a 'world-renowned conference director'? What else do you know? Or better yet, did anything you scrounge up on me not match what I've shared with you?"

"That doesn't always matter. And you knew who I was and didn't say a thing. We talked about *so much*, Cozette."

I give him a yeah-sure face scrunch. "I told you the truth about myself, and when the conversation got to too close, you changed the subject. You shared surface details. I kept thinking up horrible scenarios as to why you wouldn't talk about yourself." I regret bringing that up the moment it falls from my mouth.

He halts with his fingers on the handle of the van. His jaw is tight, face red, and I've never seen him scowl before. "Was it horrible enough for you?"

"That's not what I meant." Tears threaten, and I'm glad for the light rain and the wind whipping my hair. The silence is so long, it's impossible not to fill it. "I should have told you, but I didn't want to push if you didn't want to share. And clearly you didn't."

Not with me. He wanted to share a tiny portion—an inch when I was already four miles ahead. How did my fun Christmas romp turn into a complicated disaster? I want to hug him. It doesn't feel right not having physical contact with him. I've gotten used to it.

I take a step closer.

His glare slashes my heart. "You can't understand me...the actual me, if you meet my history and bank account first."

"I've met so many millionaires, Nico. I've worked with CEOs and high-level politicians. Your history—" I suck my lips into my mouth and take a calming breath before continuing. "It's part of who you are, as is your wealth and your choice to buy this particular paradise, but those are just portions of the whole, and I really like the whole Nico."

He rubs his hands over his face, and his exhale sounds shaky and tight. "You don't get it. I don't know you either. The person I fell—" His upper lip lifts in a grimace. "It would have been fascinating to have met as two normal people, but we didn't."

"Yes, we did. Did I make you approach me? In the grand scheme you've imagined, did I wear a corset so I could manipulate you into giving me your shirt?"

He looks toward the clouds, closing his eyes as the misting rain picks up. With a big sigh, his tilts his chin back down and squints with a puffy, red stare.

I take a breath, rubbing my forehead at the headache from lack of sleep and too many emotions. "Look, you took care of me, were kind to me. There was nothing fake about the fun we were having together. Can we bring that back, please?"

"Unfortunately, no." He shrugs. "Everything—you wanting me to be your rebound guy and the scavenger hunt. I can't take anything that happened between us for the truth. Everyone treats me differently when they know." He splays his arms wide, then lets them fall to his sides with a thwack. "Everyone."

"Oh yeah? Ilaria treats you differently? Xiamara? Did you lump them into the greedy, self-serving crowd that hurt you once, like you're doing to me? You're right—you really don't know me at all." I clutch my shirt over my heart. "I like *you*."

More than like. If he didn't mean much, I would have stayed in the room, walked back down the hall, let him go. But he doesn't want me to chase him. He's not listening to the fact that I care.

His brows furrow, and while I'd love to believe my words struck some logical chord in him, I'm afraid it's distaste in his eyes, like James always gave me during arguments.

I take two steps back and wipe my cheeks with my palms. "My mistake. Come talk to me when you realize you're being an idiot."

I spin and walk toward the building, flinching when the van door slams.

17

TRASH CASTLES IN THE SAND

The second I flop face-first on my room's couch, the tears pour. First, because I'm cold and should be in bed with my head on Nico's chest, still basking in the afterglow of our orgasm-fest, but then...then because I'm pissed.

How dare he question my morals. I would never, ever in a million years take advantage of someone like that. He has come across some serious monsters to jump to such a shit conclusion about me. About *me*! I'm mad at them too, but really, Nico? Sure, I've had men and women fawn too. Sidle up to me because of my position in the conference world, but I'm not pointing a finger at everyone who flutters their damn lashes at me, accusing them of sucking up so I'll make them my assistant or drop their name at conferences.

Criminy fuckmas, he needs to get his head out of his ass and look around. And paternity disputes? Who would tie themselves to him by using a freaking baby? I mean, it's a baby! A tiny human with thoughts and fears and hopes of love. Greedy pieces of—

Oh. What if he's a parent? Pacing from the living room to the bedroom only makes me dizzy and antsy to do something.

I flip open my laptop and search the internet for my company. Nothing but reviews and advertisements. If there's a problem, it's not public knowledge. Nico isn't ruled by fairness, that's for sure. Granted, his life hasn't been fair. While my parents were baking cookies with me, his were—. I shove the thought deep inside like it's an escaped ember from the fireplace.

He's been through unimaginable tragedy, then used for fame and fortune. Rinse and repeat. Still, he shouldn't have treated me that way. The sparks we had would have filled up the tree at Rockefeller Plaza, and he blew the damn fuse.

Does he seriously categorize me with the others? I was only trying to make him comfortable by not prying, even though it was immensely difficult. What would he have done if I told him? He would have backed away, kept to his fake fraternization policy, and I'd have spent Christmas drinking and working. If I hadn't googled him, I would have pried too hard, said the exact wrong thing, and he would have run away. Maybe that would have been for the better.

My chest seizes tight. I need to get out of this room. There are too many sexy memories staring back at me—the romped-on sheets, the counter, and box of bûche de Noël.

A shower rinses away tears, some of my muscle soreness, and Nico. I dress and call down to the main lobby to request room cleaning. They're bound to be busy cleaning up after the storm, but I can't come back to coconut and vanilla scent unless Nico is here with me.

The hallway is a fog of silence, the elevator four walls of emptiness, and even passing people in the hall is outrageously quiet. With Nico and Ilaria around, I haven't been alone much. Outside, I stop on the sand-coated patio along with other guests to study the damage with wide eyes. Employees sweat, frantically pulling sandbags from the tarps to uncover fragile flowers.

The waves still crash high on the beach. The stretch of land is rippled, dappled with shells, seaweed, and—

I dash toward the stranded, flopping little shark left behind by a wave. With a gentle grip on his tail and under his soft belly, I hoist him into the waves. A sweet familiar face a few yards down is doing the same.

Ruth stands up and summons me with a waving hand. "There are more stuck in the tide pools, and you're young."

I grab another and toss him back to the sea. A frantic yellow-striped fish gets cupped in my palms and goes back too. The other guests get the hint and join Ruth and me in our mad dash to save the creatures left behind by quickly receding waves.

After a half hour, the waves reveal nothing but sand and shells. Ruth nods in approval. "I'll keep an eye out for more, but that was the bulk of them."

"What else needs to be done?" I ask, scanning the small crowd, recognizing some faces but not the one I'm seeking.

Branches, trash, and coconuts are everywhere. The clean, perfectly manicured stretch of beach is a hot mess. Ruth brushes sandy hands on her jean capris. "It will take a few days to clean up. Staff will be busy, but they will fix it."

I snatch a bendy white branch and flex it. It's perfect for a make-believe crown or a wreath. I start weaving it in a circle and walk a few feet to grab another.

"Cozette," Linda says approaching with Phil. "Can you believe this?"

"I know," I say and wedge the knobby end of the second branch in between a wound section of the first. "I've never been through a hurricane or a tropical storm." It was a delight until it wasn't. I sniffle and keep weaving. I need to keep my mind off of Nico. Working will help.

Phil darts off to rescue another flopping fish.

"What do you have there, dear?" Ruth asks quietly as I

reach for another branch and release it from its sandy prison. I meet her worried eyes, and she steps closer, placing cool fingers on my forearm. "What happened?"

I shake my head and swallow hard. "It's fine. Would you happen to have some giveaway swag?"

After a long moment of staring at me, her concerned expression turns resigned. "Yes. What do you have in mind?"

"I have a way to help." The beach and myself. I take a step back and clear the tears from my voice. I paste on my conference grin and project loud. "Who will be the rulers of beach tidiness? The crowned royals of..." *Think, Cozette. There's a game here. Oh!* "Of the renowned trash castle competition."

Guests had already begun gathering around the four of us, but the ones starting to wander turn back and head our way.

Ruth grins. "Are you conducting a beach cleanup?"

"Is that okay?" Please say *yes*. I need to do something besides replay the last twenty-four hours on repeat.

"That would be helpful, as long as the guests remain happy and safe."

"I will try my best." I turn to the gathering crowd. "Looks like there won't be a lot of sunbathing today, but that doesn't mean the beach is off-limits. I mean, look at this wonderland." I wave my hand about at the less-than-pristine shoreline.

The response is mostly raised eyebrows and amusement, with a few latent laughers after a round of Spanish translation.

I swish my hand through the air. "You're not looking hard enough. The storm has provided us with a ton of building materials. In twenty minutes the hunt for supplies will commence, and then the contest for trash castle building will begin. Who will be crowned?" I wiggle my fingers in the air and whisper, "It's a mystery."

A couple of people clap. Good. I'm not dealing with an anti-goofiness crowd. It's happened before and is not a fun situation to be in.

I look past them at the recently pulled tarps and the workers who are unbinding the trees and checking for damage. I swear I saw Nico in my peripheral vision, but it must have been a mirage.

"Go get a snack," I say. "Change to trash collecting clothes and meet back here where the contest will begin..." I fade out my voice. "Begin...begin."

As soon as people disperse toward the building I turn to Ruth. "I can make crowns if you don't have something suitable. Is there a border they can't cross? Do you think I can use those tarps? I should see if we can get alcohol here. Everyone is so busy though—"

"Cozette, dear." She squeezes my hand to stop my rambling. "We can make it happen. Let's get started."

18

THE PERFECT FIT

I laugh as Jamal from The Clean Team and Madison from Team Trash Talk fight over a huge spiral shell. I was shocked when Madison and Joonwoo, the newlyweds from the van, came up for air and joined the competition as our sassiest-mouthed team.

"We need a turret!" Jamal says, laughing, while Madison leaps for the shell he holds above his head. He has about a foot of height on her.

"What the flip is a turret, you...you too-tall, shell-stealing schmuck?!" Madison yells between bouncing. "I need a circular, pointy tower so our structure can be a castle!"

"That *is* a turret!" He steps around her and makes a run for it, but she's quick and cuts him off.

"I found it first!" she says, arms wide as she puts up a hell of a defense.

He still holds it high. "But you put it down. Queen Cozette, Lady Ruth, we need—" He closes one eye and tips his head back and forth. "Uh, royal arbitration."

Everyone has adhered to royal-speak, which has been pure delight, even with my tanked mood. I blow my whistle, courtesy of a bin of bric-a-brac items in the storage room closet, and make the time-out sign. "There's a conflict of interest pertaining to the spiral-shelled...turret of enchantment."

Phil pops up from his octagonal castle design. "Ooh."

I hold a palm out, and Jamal hands over the shell with a disgruntled sigh.

"To settle the dispute, we shall have a talent show of weirdness. Both contestants will perform their oddest trick for the other teams and our captive audience." I wave to Peter with his tray of drinks, and he bows his head in return.

The other competitors approach as Jamal and Madison stretch like they're warming up for a boxing match. They're in it to win it. The last few hours of tossing myself into this task has helped derail thoughts of Nico but not entirely escape them. I look for him around every corner. Catch glimpses of his phantom just to lose sight. He's probably here, cleaning up, working. How is he handling everything? When am I going to see him again?

When things get quiet, I get invasive snippets of how his fingers shook this morning when he cupped my face, how last night he held me like he'd done so for years while he pulsed inside me.

"You've got this, baby," Fatima tells Jamal and claps her hands.

"Come on, Mads, you know what to do." Joonwoo nods at his wife.

She smiles knowingly, a plan of action twinkling in her eyes.

"Defender first," I yell. "You're up, Jamal."

He hums, then blows a long raspberry in a rising vocal scale. That's it? He clears his throat, then sings...opera. His projection makes me cover my heart with my hand and forget to breathe. It's a wall of sound that reaches higher and higher until he hits a note that would have made Freddie Mercury cry with exultation.

When he stops, we all blink, then go nuts with applause.

"Yeah, that's right," Fatima yells, pumping her arm. "You should hear him in the shower. Oh baby. Mmm."

I laugh at their sweetness, and attention turns to Team Trash Talk. Madison's lips form an O with her intake of breath. She stretches her neck, then her right arm. Circles her shoulders as she blows that held breath out with puffed cheeks.

"That's the way, Mads." Joonwoo claps, crouched and watching closely.

She does this odd shimmy, rolls her shoulder, bends her arm behind her, and licks her freaking elbow.

"What the—" I yell over the cheering crowd. "I didn't think that was possible!"

She smiles and does it again to clarify that she can indeed do a very weird thing.

I blow my whistle to quiet the crowd. "Okay, okay, that was some serious stuff, folks. Let's vote." I lift Jamal's arm, and a few people raise their hands.

"That wasn't odd, Jamal. It was outstanding," Phil says, clapping but not casting his vote.

Jamal shrugs with a grin.

When I lift Madison's, hands shoot in the air. It was a weird contest after all.

I hand the shell over, and she jumps up and down and gets kiss-attacked by Joonwoo as if she just won a year's supply of ice cream. They sprint off to their spot in the line of wood, shell, and trash castles. Jamal gets claps on the back, hugs, and fields questions about his singing.

Some teams head toward Peter for more drinks, and others dive back into their work.

"It's been a long day." Ruth appears beside me. "You need a break. Go eat."

"I'm not hungry." I've been eating with Nico for the last few days, and being alone seems impossibly final.

Her gaze burns a hole in the side of my head. Ruth knows things. Sees everything like she has X-ray vision, revealing thoughts instead of bones. I roll my teary eyes and shrug. "I heard he was the owner when I arrived. He found out and didn't take it well. Accusations were made."

"Oh dear," she says and puts a hand on my shoulder, giving it a light squeeze. "He's..." She squints. "Some things aren't easy for him. He'll come around."

I wipe at my eyes. Stupid tears. I just met the guy. Being away from him shouldn't be this hard, but I wish I knew where he was and if he's come to grips with his idiocy yet, because I need to fold myself into his arms and smell him.

"Come on. Break time. We eat, then we come back." She loops her hand in the crook of my arm and tugs. "Help an old lady."

I give up and hand my whistle over to Linda, who gives me a questioning glance but stays quiet.

Even through washing our hands in the first-floor bathroom and gathering fruit and tamales from the buffet, Ruth remains silent. As I don't know what else to say, I follow suit.

Once we settle into seats, she smiles. "He's had a hard life, Cozette."

"I know. I was a terrible person and looked him up, just a little."

"Ah. I see." She takes a bite and sips from a cup of tea, leaving a fuchsia half-moon on the rim. "You're not after his money, are you?"

"No," I snap. Other diners glance our way, and I wipe my mouth with my blue cloth napkin to hide. "Sorry. No, I'm not. I can take care of myself. I like him. We were having fun, but this is for the better. I'm leaving the day after tomorrow. It's an easier break."

"Oh, I don't know about that. You seem..." She flicks her fingers toward me. "It's not easy for you, is it?"

I fight tears hard, but I can't stop the tightening muscles in my face, the gasps my lungs refuse to hold in. I hold up a finger and rush off to the bathroom again.

The left-most stall is a good hiding place. I slam the door, lean against the wall, and blot at my tears with toilet paper. How does this hurt so much? He was molten-warm, then dunked me in ice and I'm not thawing out anytime soon. I'm so mad at him right now and every stupid person who molded him into this mistrusting mess. He really can't see that I'm not like that? I thought he knew me better than this.

But he doesn't. It's been days, and neither of us has had enough time to understand each other, especially with how secretive he's been. It was a mistake, I think. At least, letting my emotions go beyond the rebound zone was a mistake. It was lust. I should appreciate the moment and move along. I can be with other people. Yay for me and thank you, Nico.

Thanks for being the comparison for all jesting wit and sexy times from now on. Ugh. I drop my face in my hands.

Enough of this. The contestants need me. I have a—no it's not a job, but I have something to focus on besides Nico. Deep breaths. In. Out.

When I return to the table, Ruth is talking on the phone in German. I haven't a clue what she's saying, but I have an idea who she may be talking to—and that isn't going to help the situation, since Nico already thinks I'm manipulating others. When I sit, she says something and hangs up.

"If that was Nico, I'm not going to be happy. No more talk about him either. I'm all done."

She purses her lips and sips her tea. "Eat, dear. We have trashy castles to judge. That was a brilliant idea. There are gift certificates to the gift shop at the front desk for the second and third place winners, and a couples massage for the winners."

Aw. "Really?"

"Yes. You've managed to keep the guests happy and clean up the beach in record time. You should work here."

Yeah, about that...I swallow a bite of tamale without tasting it, eyes to the ceiling to keep my tears from falling, and then stand. "I already have a job. Let's go."

After two more hours of collection and building, the bystanders have grown in number and we have twelve structures, from trash cabins to a four-foot-tall driftwood fortress. Contestants take photos next to their masterpieces. The teams mingle, talking animatedly, a far difference from the quiet collection of supplies earlier in the day.

This was my favorite part of conferences—how strangers come together and get to know each other with team building exercises or after-hours sharing. We wouldn't have known someone could lick their elbow or sing opera, and now a group is standing around belly laughing while they try in every way to mimic Madison. Forget shallow chats about the weather and business trends, playing is what bonds people. I've missed conducting games in person.

Phil and Linda, Team Takeout, secure third for their use of seaweed, making their castle look like the Moss Monster's paradise.

Team Trash Talk takes second and jumps around, trash talking everyone about how their magic shell circular tower thingy is the bomb.

Once we stop laughing, we crown The Tidy Tonis Team, a quiet gay couple. Tonya and Antoinette both went by Toni when they met. They built an impressive woven sculpture with the same thin, bendy branches I used to make crowns and added a nice amount of trash to make doorways and turrets. The roofs are domed with coconuts.

Ruth kisses my cheek and tells me her old bones need a rest. I thank her for her assistance orchestrating before we're overtaken by the teams with hugs. I'm dragged inside for drinks and celebration karaoke. I try to get out of it, but the women cart me off to the restroom for a quick cleanup, Linda making sure I'm never more than a foot from her, preventing my escape.

Everywhere I've been today, I've scanned for Nico like he'd be there to walk up, grasp my hand, and tug me away with him. By the time Walt hands me a drink and Jose pulls people up to dance, I give up. Nico is not interested.

After another hour of chatter and one drink, I say goodnight to the group as they dance in happy, matched pairs.

My room looks as it did on day one, except for the box of remaining bûche de Noël and the bobblehead. It smells like flowers. I rinse the day's grime off my body and climb into bed with my laptop and the remaining cake.

I don't have any new requests, which isn't entirely odd as it's the day after Christmas, though I had four requests last year at this time. I'm left with my seven and get to work, researching locations in the States and using online features to set up catering for the smaller meetings. I settle back into the pillows and create spreadsheet after spreadsheet from the template I designed on the plane ride to prepare for the new year. I'll have an influx of clients soon and hopefully some repeat clients where I can cut and paste from previous years.

The amount of work I could have this year gives me a little thrill. If my projections are correct, I'll be busy. Not as much as I used to do, but enough.

I can handle it.

19

WORK IT OUT

I wake up with a start. My fingers still touch the keys of my laptop, but the screen is black. A squint in the direction of the clock tells me it's four in the morning. Setting my laptop aside, I roll over, but a buzz in the distance vibrates my nerves. I slide from the bed and amble to the kitchen to fish my phone from the drawer, where it lives now because Nico hasn't contacted me, but James keeps sending sweet notes.

There are text messages on my phone from James and from my parents.

I miss you. James texts. *You always made Christmas special. Was yours good?*

Growling, I swipe that aside to unpack later and read the messages from my parents. They have a pre-dawn flight out of Quebec. The renters left yesterday, and the cleaning crew came through last night. They let Dad know that the house was still standing and the renters only minimally assaulted the couch.

I huff a laugh and text them back. *I'm flying out tomorrow. Can I come home?*

James is expecting me back in New York, but I'm not ready.

Why are you awake? Dad texts back. *Of course. Did you change your flight?*

Not yet. I'll do that, then go back to sleep.

Sleep well, little Caroliner.

Dad likes it when I'm home. New York can wait until I'm good and ready. I don't want to see James when I'm still upset about Nico, though I have no urge to run into James's arms or anything. I guess I am over him.

I check departure times. There's nothing available. A phone call to the airport confirms that all flights are full, but they take my information for a stand-by anytime from now until departure time tomorrow. The return flight tomorrow is nonstop, so I can't even skip out in Charlotte or Pittsburgh. Looks like I may be heading to New York after all. I'm tempted to call in Helena again. She's proven herself a travel miracle worker.

I lie back and close my eyes, but sleep won't come. The room feels too big without Nico in it. It's beautiful but lacking, too quiet and chilly. Every time I shift, my muscles protest, reminding me of how close he and I were. We had a good time.

Dragging my phone out, I see James has sent more messages. *Are you coming home tomorrow? To New York?*

If my parents wouldn't freak out if they couldn't get in touch with me, this tie to James would take a dip in the pool. I shove it back in the drawer. He's a problem for back-in-the-States Cozette.

When the sky lightens outside, I dress, reluctantly free my phone, and walk down to the ocean with a cup of coffee. Nico isn't around this morning. I hope he's okay.

Wet sand sucks me deeper with each wave lapping over my ankles. Nature holds its breath, and then the sun rises. I stare at it until it burns my sore eyes and I'm forced to look away.

I can't do nothing. I cave, take a long moment to stare at Nico's goofy contact picture, then text him. *The sunrise is pretty this morning. I enjoyed spending Christmas with you.*

With heavy feet and an empty cup, I go back to my room, change into my bikini, grab my laptop, and set up shop on a lounger under some palm trees. I drink coconut water and dive back into work. I simultaneously organize all client tasks in a rhythm—location, technology, food, repeat, again and again. Then I analyze all clients, tossing those who will probably have a similar event this upcoming year. I make folders for them too.

No one bothers me, though I'm so tunneled into my task, if someone approached, they would have to throw something at me to get my attention.

There are still no new requests, but everything seems fine with the company. They aren't blasting social media like they usually do, but it's the holidays. That will rev back up in the new year. I'm sure.

I peek at job openings in North Carolina. There are several, including a lower-level spot at my old company. Could I go back? I stretch my legs and wiggle my bare toes. I'd have to go back to suits and heels again. No more weekends or nights of relaxation.

My stomach growls and I run inside to make a late breakfast plate, then carry it back to my lounger. When I get back to the States, I'll have to confirm a few things by phone for these clients, but they will all have organized, stress-free events. I check my work website, but there are no more requests. The waves kiss the shore as couples parade by, hand in hand.

Nico's not going to talk to me before I leave. He's hidden himself away and will ghost me until I go home. That stings more than it should. It was always meant to be temporary. A fun and distracting holiday in a paradise. I take a long walk along the water, stopping to pick up pretty shells. The farther I get from the hotel, the wilder and more natural the landscape becomes.

I plop down on the sand and watch the rough waters mosh. North Carolina will be good until I figure out where I should end up. With my job, I can work anywhere. Maybe I'll explore for a while, checking out cities I don't know on mini-vacations until I find where I fit.

A figure walks toward me, and I squint into the sun. After a few minutes, Ruth sits beside me. "Hello, dear. Enjoying your alone time?"

I smile. "Yes, but this is better."

She rubs my shoulder. "Will you tell me how you came to be an event guru?"

"Well..." I start from the beginning and end with my new plan that I figured out just now. I'm going to visit my virtual clients when I can, and while I'm visiting new locations, I'll figure out where I belong. I miss meeting new people, and I didn't realize how much until now. I nod. "Yes. That's the plan."

"It's...a good plan." Her voice lacks sincerity. She draws a wave shape in the sand with a finger, her thin skin patterned with wrinkles. "What Henry and I had was so unique, Cozette, and when I see that spark in others..." She turns her face to me. "It reminds me of him. I want to lock those two together, because they shouldn't miss a minute apart. There's never enough time when it's the right fit."

"So subtle, Ms. Ruth." I share a sad smile with her. "I can fix a lot of things, but not this." And my track record for fixing things with men is zero. I push, try, and fail.

We sit in silence for a long while, letting thoughts ebb and flow with the ocean. Ruth's presence is nice, but I'm probably keeping her from her job. I brush myself off and offer a hand to help her up. We head back toward the hotel.

"Is Ilaria okay?" I ask. I haven't heard from her so I'm not sure if she's just avoiding the drama, or if she's busy because it's midday right after a tropical storm. I hope Nico didn't lay into her too badly if he figured out that she's the one who spilled.

"She's upset," Ruth says. "And worried about you."

"And Nico, I'm sure."

Ruth squeezes my hand. "About the two of you." Before I can scoff at that, she releases me. "Come to the club tonight for drinks. I will send you off with dreadful karaoke, and the boys will want dances."

"Fine, but I'm not getting drunk. I've had my one allocated hangover day, and I have flights tomorrow."

We part, and I go up to my room to call Ilaria. She knocks within minutes, and when I wave her in, she's quiet with a guilty puppy look in her eyes.

I fidget with the hem of my shorts. "I'm sorry if there's drama from…" I swish my hand through the air. "Everything."

She leaps to hug me. "I'm sorry, Cozette. He's just…he doesn't handle things well."

"You think?" I give her a squeeze and release her. "Can you take me to him?" I'd like to see him if only to make sure he's fine and to say goodbye.

She grimaces "No. I'm sorry." She rubs her forehead and sniffles. "I really am, Cozette. I blame myself here and—"

I take her hand and squeeze. "Not your fault. If he won't talk to me, that's on him, not you." Before I can break down, I grab the bobblehead from the kitchen counter. "Give this to him to do whatever with."

"I will. I'm sorry, Cozette. This is your holiday and, ugh."

"It's really okay. I had an amazing time, and I'm fine. I'm headed to New York in the morning, and I'll get back to work. It's fine. This place is paradise. I've really enjoyed myself, even on rum punch night. Dancing with Jose and Walt was fun. Ruth is wonderful. You're amazing, and Xiamara—"

"Cozette," she sneaks in through my rant. "I wish things were different."

I nod. "Me too. Anyway, if I don't see you, I want you to know I appreciate you. I'm not allowed to tip you unless that's a fake rule too, but if I could, I'd tip you a bunch."

She gives me an odd glance. "No. No tipping is allowed. Fake rule?"

"Nico told me when I arrived that there was a no guest fraternization policy. If you visit New York, you better call me."

She frowns. "I will."

We finish our goodbyes, and my phone rings as I'm walking to the bedroom. There's an opening on a flight to Charlotte. It leaves at three in the morning. I wrinkle my nose but accept the flight and call the airport situated on the island. A perky woman answers, and I tell her my predicament, inquiring if there's a flight going to San Juan airport between now and midnight. There is. Guests from the private huts on the other side of the island are flying out in about an hour. Do I need a ride to the airport?

Yes, please, and thank you.

As I pack up, I recap my whirlwind vacation. I could have done more. I'd like to see the waterfalls, and Nico said the parasailing and kayaking are incredible, but then there were storms of the nature and the Nico variety. If things had been different, I would have liked to stay longer. This is the kind of place someone needs to come to for a couple of weeks. Week one, settle in. Gain your island legs with rum, food, hammocks, and a simple adventure or two, then roll into exploration mode. A two-week relax and adventure trip. I can see the brochure and—

I have got to stop eventing all over everyone.

My phone buzzes. It's a text message telling me my ride will be here in five minutes.

This time, I shove additional clothing into my laptop bag, including Nico's shirt, which I try not to think too hard about. With the new garments, everything is packed so tight, it wouldn't shock me if there was a clothing explosion from my teal suitcase at any time. I carefully stack everything—suitcase, carry-on, laptop bag, and pillow—as if working with a bomb.

Hoping I got everything, I blow a quick kiss to this beautiful room and sprint downstairs.

Jennifer is at the front desk today and greets me with a huge grin. "Hello, Ms. Fay."

"Hi, I need to—"

"Hello, my most beautiful American flower," Jose says, walking up behind me. "Are you headed to dinner?" His blazing grin falters. "You look sad, darling."

I nearly choke on the knot in my throat. I'm going to miss this place and these people so much. We exchange kisses on both cheeks, and he holds my shoulders at arm's length.

"I'm checking out," I say.

A van pulls up outside the glass doors. The lettering on the side says, *The Cliffs*.

Jose stares out the door and gives a small wave to the driver as I turn to address Jennifer. "I need to pay my bill—sign something or whatever."

She taps on her computer, lips in a straight line. "I hope you enjoyed yourself here."

"It was wonderful," I say. "Everyone is so nice." Jose sidles up to me, and I squeeze his hand.

Jennifer's brows furrow. "Oh. Your room and charges have been comped."

I straighten my spine, even with the weight of my bags. "I'm sorry?" No way. He knows I was completely joking when I told him he could deduct my advising bills from the room.

After more clicks and reading she smiles. "Yes. You have a zero balance. We will miss—"

"Nuh uh. What was the balance before it was comped?"

I'm not taking some consolation prize or falling into whatever stupid trap Nico has set for me as he tries to prove what a terrible person I am. I don't want a cent of his damn money.

"Oh, um, two thousand, seven hundred and ten dollars, including gift shop items."

I slap my card on the desk. "Great. Run this through for that amount."

"Oh, well—"

"Do it, Jennifer," I say, too harsh. "Please and thank you. I'll be right back."

Jose grabs my suitcase and follows me out the door. We're greeted by the driver, a woman with dreads and a leather hat.

"Hey, I saw you riding a horse when we drove in on Saturday."

"You did?" she asks, her handshake warm but not as much as her beaming face. "Hermes and I trot the island daily. I'm Vic. You must be Cozette."

She grabs my bags and with Jose's help uses mad Tetris skills to organize them in the back. Jose stays oddly sullen and silent, only speaking when Vic talks about the tropical storm. They lost the roof of a hut, but it needed replacing anyway. There are four other people loaded into the van. A few turn to smile and wave.

I run back in and get my card from Jennifer, sign the receipt, and nearly face-plant Jose.

"Did you have fun here?" he asks.

Why does he look so sad? "Of course I did." I swallow hard and hug him. "You and Walt are amazing. You really make this place a blast. I'm going to miss you all. Tell him bye for me. Oh, and Ruth and..." *And Nico.* "Just tell everyone I said bye."

"Ahem," Vic says, leaning in the doorway. She waves at Jennifer, then scrunches her eyes at Jose, wrinkles from the corners of her eyes stretching to her hairline. "Stop blocking my passenger, dancer man, we got a journey."

He hugs me back. "I will. Take care, Cozette. Come see us again sometime."

What's with everyone going all serious on me? Am I being the same way? Maybe I'm projecting a bad mood or something.

I toss on a wide grin and salsa backward. He takes the bait

and leaps forward to spin me toward the door. I blow him a kiss when he releases me and head toward the passenger seat.

"Front seat if you want," Vic says. "It's a short trip."

The van is older than El Escape's one. It has a key and doesn't smell new or like coconuts and vanilla, but I won't hold that against it because it's getting me to the airport. The passengers in the two rows behind me smile and wave again. "Hi," I say. "Thanks for the ride." El Escape gets smaller as we drive away.

"Happy to help our neighbors. We're one big happy family on Simona Island." She grins wide and turns past the blue sign.

Her statement sends a thread of relief through me, relaxing the tightness in my shoulders. Nico doesn't have family, but he found one here. I'm glad for him. "Well, I appreciate it."

"We're headed to the airport," Vic says, punching the ceiling, making two thunks. "Did you all relax?"

"Yes," the group cheers as one.

"What was your favorite part?"

I like her enthusiasm. She'd be able to get a crowd going, but in a want-to-participate way, not a demand-it-whether-people-want-to-or-not way.

A sunburned guy tosses his arm over the man next to him. "Cliff diving."

The Asian woman in the back seat claps her hands. "I loved that. We're coming back to do that again, yes?"

The man next to her rubs dark fingers over his mouth. "No way. I can't believe you got me to do it once." His voice is a deep, purring baritone.

"That sounds fun," I say. I wonder if the staff of El Escape jump from cliffs on their days off. Fourteen square miles is a lot of acreage for three tourist locations. There are a few houses scattered off the main road, but they're tucked between thick trees. I bet there's a town and residential housing somewhere. Condos on the beach maybe.

We come to a stretch of road I recognize. Sure enough, the red-painted pole sticks out of the sand marking the place Nico and I snorkeled.

Vic honks the horn in a quick song. Beep, beep...beep beep beep. "Say goodbye to Mr. Lopez, everyone."

The group waves toward the trees.

"Thanks for sharing this awesome island, Mr. Lopez," the woman from the back says.

"He shares the island?" I ask the window. Oh...the old man in the pink house is... "He's the owner of the island?"

"Yep," Vic says. "Sweetness alive that man is. He named the island after his late wife. They used to come around and visit us when Simona was alive. Said they wanted to share paradise with the world, a few people at a time, and that watching others fall in love with the best place on Earth was their joy."

Why would Nico keep that to himself? Maybe because van drivers don't have access to island owners' backyards. He tried hard to keep up the ruse. I shake my head and half-listen to the activities everyone has participated in over the last couple of weeks.

Turns out Vic owns a series of private huts on the beach and in the water on the other side of the island that focus on adventure outings. They have a clubhouse that guests come to for food and activities, but it's more secluded from other guests. She sends the socialites and spa goers to El Escape, and in return they send people concerned with quiet but wanting to stay active to The Cliffs. There's also a jungle campground with tree houses.

Maybe one day, long from now, I'll return and check out what I missed.

Unlike Nico, Vic happily accepts my tip, hugs us all, and sends us to the tiny plane. Once I'm settled in, my throat tightens and my eyes ache. This was a beautiful escape. I won't see another Simona Island sunrise from that location. I should have said goodbye to Ruth. Linda and Phil were leaving tomorrow too. We were going to take the shuttle together.

While the flight attendant goes through safety procedures and checks our straps, I stare at my phone with a thousand things I want to say to Nico.

I'm sorry such terrible things happened to you. I hope one day, someone proves you wrong and you find happiness.

Still five stars.

The pilot announces that it's time to put away our phones. With shaking fingers, I turn it off without writing a single word and hug my decorative travel pillow.

Goodbye, Nico.

20

NO MORE CHASING

Mom and Dad pick me up from the airport at eleven in the morning and ask if I'm hungry. I've been traveling for the good part of a day and had spiked coffee for dinner last night. Yeah, I'm hungry.

When we pull into our favorite hamburger joint, I break down crying, and Dad quickly turns toward the house instead.

Mom crawls over the console and sits in the back seat with me, holding my hand while I tell them in broken cry words that Nico loves hamburgers and I may love Nico and that's stupid because it's been days, but I don't have to worry about it anymore because it's over between us. He's there. I'm here, and he won't talk to me.

I finish by telling them that I had a fantastic time and sob-laugh.

Mom tucks me under her arm, and Dad squeezes the steering wheel in rhythm, squeaking the leather.

I kick his seat. "Don't be mad at him, he's had a rough time. He was sweet to me."

"He better have been." He grumbles something under his breath.

"I've never seen you angry at a guy for me, Dad."

He sighs and pulls into the garage. "You've never reacted like this to someone before."

They get me inside and make me a sandwich, which makes me upset all over again, because how many times has Nico needed a sandwich and no one was there to make him one?

Though I'd slept on the plane, it wasn't restful and three nights of barely-sleep caught up. When I regain consciousness in my childhood room, my phone is chiming loudly. Everything is blurry.

"Yeah?" I answer in the middle of a yawn.

"Cozette?"

I shoot up so fast, I waver with dizziness. "Nico?"

"You left." He sounds tired too.

I rub my eyes and glare at the clock. Quarter to two in the afternoon. That was an enjoyable cat nap. "Well, yeah. Guests tend to do that."

"That's not...I mean, you left early."

My bearings are nowhere to be found. "Um. I did."

"You just woke up."

"You are really observant today." I yawn again.

He chuckles, but it's not his carefree tone. It's an awkward uncertainty that makes me tighten my lips. The silence is uncommon between us.

"What do you need, Nico?" Does he want to throw a couple more accusations at me, or has he come to grips with his idiocy?

"Um." There's a lengthy breath through the line. "I blew up and...it wasn't right to blame you. Ilaria told me everything that happened before, uh, *us*. I'd like you to come back to Simona Island."

That is pretty close to an apology. However, he wants *me* to come back? It's way too early for this. Or late for that matter.

"I don't even know you," I whisper.

"You know I like eggplant and recycling. I know you like brussels sprouts and holidays. That's a good start. Come back and we can get to know each other."

We could. I'd fly down, he'd pick me up at the airport, and we'd start again. It's so easy to picture because that's what I do. I follow, I sacrifice, I try.

I shake my head as if he can see me. "I'm so tired of chasing boys. You all want to push the responsibility of working things out onto me and I'm done. 'Don't leave, Cozette. Come home, Cozette. Go home, come back...' You know what? No. I'm going to do my thing. You want me? Come find me." I hang up with an irritated fingerpoke.

Oh, my shit, what did I just do?

I grab a pillow and scream into it. The phone in my palm is dark and silent. Will he call me back? Ask where I'm at? I'm wide awake now and want to call him back, but I won't because that would only prove my point. Wrapping my fingers around my tangible tie to Nico, I exit the bed and amble to the coffeepot. Warmed-up coffee is still coffee.

The house is quiet and scented with the cinnamon pinecones my mom decorates with during the winter. It's the scent of every Christmas. My parents put up the fake balsam but left off the personal ornaments. They treated decorations scattered over every surface the same way. Generic boughs of holly and Santa statues, but none of the vintage cottages and O-mouthed carolers that have celebrated the season through our family's generations.

The only near-and-dear item displayed is the huge Christmas carousel on the walnut buffet in the dining room. The saddled polar bear's leg goes the wrong way from when I shook its paw a little too rough. At eight years old, I'd just learned how to use superglue.

I wonder if Nico has items from his parents, or if he walked away from his family home and never looked back. I'm not sure what I would do in his situation, and thinking about it makes my lungs tighten. I divert my attention to sip coffee and wander the main floor. It's too clean. No newspapers on the side table or fishing rods next to the door. My parents really tidied for the renters. When I sit in my grandfather's rocking chair, Mom and Dad walk in, tennis rackets in hand.

"Good afternoon," Dad announces long and loud. "You didn't sleep long."

I lift my cup in greeting.

"Get dressed," Mom says with a grin. "We're going ice skating, then to dinner, then a movie."

"You two don't have to—"

"Zip," she says pinching the air. "Get dressed. Barbeque awaits."

I rock myself out of the chair. "Well, if barbeque is involved, I guess I have to. Let me check work emails first." I thumb through my phone. Still no requests. I go to the main site, and everything seems fine except there hasn't been a new sign-up since the two I accepted a few days before Christmas. That makes a rock of dread settle into my stomach.

Ice skating is a zippy change of motion, the barbeque worthy of sonnets that works to mostly distract me from Nico nonsense, postponing New York problems, and whipping me away from work worries. Mostly. Except the chill reminds me of the tan now tinting my cheeks. I bet Phil and Linda are in feet of snow but soul-warmed through and through.

By the time the movie lets out and we settle back home, it's dark and I'm worn out. I turn my phone back on and wait, holding my breath. James texted me a few times wanting to know when I'd be there, some unknown number wants to repair my credit rating, and there are no others. I open the previous exchange of messages with Nico just in case, but no...nothing.

As usual, I'm worthy of being beckoned, but not enough to follow. Whatever.

I open my laptop on the canary yellow desk that's been in my room since I was ten.

I have thirty-five emails. What the hell? The contact from clients range from curious to belligerent because of a warning they have on their account. All events must be completed by Wednesday, January 2nd?

"What. Is. Happening?" I ask my empty room. Skipping to the beginning of the email boom, I find an important announcement email from the company with a *confirm receipt* tag. It states that due to unforeseen circumstances, the company is shutting down, effective immediately. They apologize for any inconvenience—of course they do—and have sent emails to all active and previous clients—of course they have.

"Dammit!" I kick the leg of my desk, then pat the surface in apology.

Mom peeks in, holding a cup of tea. "Everything okay? Did Nico call?"

"No and no." I growl as I go through emails, then open a document to make a generic announcement telling my current clients that I plan to complete all event planning by the 2nd, that I was unaware of any company issues and will be reaching out soon with personalized progress updates. The irony isn't lost on me that Nico warned me. How did he know? The phone is a magnet, pulling me to contact him. I shake my head at it as though it can see me.

Mom sets the tea down next to me and drags the gray armchair over. She reads over my shoulder and gasps. "Oh, okay. Do you need help with this?"

I give a pitchy laugh. "I need wine and another weekday." If

I hadn't done so much that last day in Simona Island, I'd be royally screwed.

"Wine I can do," Mom says, holding a finger up and standing.

I send my email, hoping that my clients will read it over the weekend and won't panic more than they already are. Opening the desk drawer, I eye my clean whiteboard. I grab a dry-erase marker and stand up. "It's been a while, old friend."

My list gets my panicked thoughts in order from biggest fire to smallest. *Complete client needs in order of intake, update résumé, send résumé to known contacts, create event timeline for each client, research potential employers, drop off résumés.* I add a box to each task to check off.

"Oh hell," Dad says, handing me a glass of red. "She's brought out the big guns."

"Ha, ha..." I let that last 'ha' fly until I run out of air. "Yeah, well, I'm going to need it to fix this mess."

Because I'm me, I smile. I love fixing messes.

21

SUIT UP

On Saturday, my phone buzzes against my ear while I'm talking to client number three. When I convince them that I haven't stolen their money and run off to the tropics—I had to cover my mouth to keep from laughing at that—we hang up and I check to see who reached out.

Nico's message makes my lungs still along with the halted, tunneled air. *When you asked me if I wanted to talk about my ex with you, I lied. I really did.*

I stare at his words, rereading a hundred times. His text is an olive branch, a question masked as a statement, a test, but not a malicious one. He's throwing pebbles at my closed window. Should I open it? I put my phone on my desk and bring my knees up, hugging them tight as I think.

I could claim he's just a guy I met on an escape vacation. That he was a temporary, easy, and not to-be-continued one-night stand. But it's Nico.

Unfolding myself from the chair, I grab my phone and reread a couple more times before responding, *I would have listened.*

I know.

No other messages come as I call other clients, finish up most confirmations for catering, and make timeline guides so clients will know exactly what to do on event day. Maybe him reaching out was a goodbye message. One of those thoughts that emerges as the mind grasps that this is the grand finale. Like how we reminisce the good things of the year right before midnight on December 31st even if six months ago we were wading through impossible knee-high mud. Those little rainbow memories burst through when the storm is over.

In the late hours of the night, as I war with my heavy eyelids while reviewing my game plan for tomorrow, my phone buzzes again.

When I was nine, Mor (mom) took me to America for a science philanthropy conference. I had my first cheeseburger at a diner in Chicago while I read the comics from the newspaper. It was one of my favorite days. I wanted to tell you that, but instead shut my mouth until you elegantly changed the subject for me.

I drain my teacup and take a long, exposed breath as I tap fingers over the screen. *Did you like the comics?*

I packed so many in my suitcase, I wore a triple set of clothes on the plane. Your coat fiasco reminded me of that moment. I laid in the snow when we got off the jet.

Imagining little Nico throwing himself in a snowbank because he was burning up is an outstanding visual. *I would have done that too*, I respond.

You would have made snow angels.

He's right. I bite my lip and swallow a lump in my throat. Is he really ready to share more? Only one way to find out. *What did your mom do?*

She sat beside me in her favorite red wool coat and laughed. Sleep well, Cozi.

The ache makes me clutch my shirt over my heart. *You too*, I text back. I didn't build a picture of Nico's family, and while there had been a small photo of them in the batch when I googled his name, I wasn't prepared for his mother to be...a person. Obviously, she was a person, but his silence and avoidance made her nonexistent. If she was like Nico though, I think we would have been good friends.

I wake Sunday to two messages.

You are coming back, right? from James. I don't even open the message. Only glare at it on my home screen. But then...*Good Morning, Cozi.* That one I open and reread a time or forty.

At least they're both not asking me to come to them. Is Nico enjoying a beautiful Simona Island sunrise, coffee cup in hand as an orange sun bursts over the bluegreen water? I can practically smell the salt and him. Deep breath. I have so much to do.

I toss out another six résumés to the industry leaders I'm familiar with, except for the place that broke me, though they will get word and reach out. That remains a last option. I'm not sure if I'm ready to take on the corporate world again, and I don't want to skip another five years then shatter into pieces, but I have to work. And I have to finish up the job I have for one more day.

I wanted to snatch your phone when I took our picture and send it to myself, Nico texts as I'm stuffing my face with a sandwich and crossing off tasks on the whiteboard. *Even though I knew it wasn't a moment I'd forget.*

For twenty minutes I wait, unable to finish my sandwich, staring at the photo of us on my phone. We look good together. Happy, except Nico's eyes are tight with a hint of worry or maybe confusion, but they're on me instead of the phone. I wasn't even running away or staring back, asking for his gaze. He saw me from moment one, and whether by accident or design, we had important time together that he fought, lost himself to, and then he panicked. I send it to him.

I'm fighting a grin when my phone buzzes an hour later, but the message makes the flickering warmth running through me turn to icicles. *I cannot fucking believe you,* James writes. I'm sure my lack of communication is frustrating. He's made his wants known, but the message is shockingly harsh coming from him.

My blank brain can't formulate a response, but then another email dings on my computer with an all-caps subject line. *I DON'T KNOW WHAT TO DO HERE!!!* Client number five is not handling our parting well. I put my phone down like it may bite. Later. I'll deal with James later.

※

It was a long weekend that's rolled into a long Monday. I walk out of Designed Corporate Events, and my shoulders slump. My feet hurt from my black heels. How odd that I used to wear them for eighteen hours straight, and now two hours is pure hell. I want my flip-flops back but it's freezing.

The square, brick building is like any other corporate office—structured with long hours and attitudes as stuffy as my suit. I'm still jaded, but this location is the best option in the area if I want to stay in North Carolina, and they want me. Ten minutes after I sent my résumé, on a New Year's Eve Monday no less, the recruiter called me and asked me to come in immediately. They would make time. I finished solidifying my events, sent my completion emails, got gussied up to corporate standards, checked my phone for texts four thousand times—received none—and took the hour drive.

After a ten-minute conversation with the manager, he carted me off to the CEO, a gray-haired black woman with dull, tired eyes. She became more animated as we talked, going from looking like she needed a nap to leaning forward, and switching from polite layman's terms to blunt industry ones. She asked if my old job knew I was on the market, and a hungry, determined twinkle hit her eyes at my answer. It made a knot form in my stomach. I'm in.

I didn't expect anyone to be working today, which was a

mistake. Events thrive during holidays. I've repressed the memories, which slides unease into my already chaotic thoughts. I'm not ready for this, but I have to be, and it's better to leap. I won't have to painfully slide into the boiling pot if I hit the bubbles at a breakneck speed. Besides, every time I stop moving, my world spins. This, I can control.

No more messages that make me frown from James, and no more messages that make me smile from Nico. It's possible I made my parents text me to make sure my phone was functioning. Twice.

I chuck my shoes at the passenger's seat as soon as I open the door, then blast the floor heat and drive home. Well, my parents' house. Until I find my place in the world, they will be my home base. Parents are amazing like that.

Tonight, we will open champagne and snack on oysters, shellfish, and tapenade. We will hug and kiss cheeks at midnight, go to bed, and start a fresh year tomorrow. Nico told me he will be transporting vacationers to an open beach near the Jungle Huts. They will have a small bonfire, sing, and eat from coolers and a makeshift grill, then set off fireworks that can be seen from most places on the island. Everyone will cheer at the end, even the poo-throwing monkeys eyeing the leftover food from the forest line. Nico scrunched his nose when he told me that part, and the memory makes me smile. We'd been lying in the hotel bed, his hand stroking patterns on my back as I sprawled over him, not wanting an inch separating us. And now we're parted by a little over two thousand miles.

I pull into the driveway and check my phone, but there's nothing but a thank-you-for-your-service email from my job and another message from client five with bullet point questions about the itinerary I sent yesterday.

The pressure of my pumps on sore feet makes me groan. Navigating the old brick path is a test of lady ninja skills.

Stilettos and crevices do not mix. I walk inside and trip when the looped front entrance rug catches my heel.

"Shoes are stupid," I yell, wiggling my foot out of the stabbing trap while slipping out of my coat.

"Yeah, they are," Nico says from the kitchen doorway.

22

NEGOTIATIONS

*M*y head shoots up so fast, I bump into the wall and lean there so I don't flop on the floor. Nico stands tall in the kitchen doorway wearing a thick knit sweater, jeans, and boots, holding a rocks glass of amber liquid. He looks good in winter attire.

Dad steps next to him with a smile and squeezes Nico's shoulder. "Hello, daughter of mine. Did they offer you the job yet?"

Nico's lips thin, and he takes a sip from his glass.

"Not...yet." I clear my throat, eyes still on Nico. "You're here."

"Now who's observant?" He smirks, and I swear if he bites that lip, I'm going to tackle him.

I take my remaining shoe off and hold the pair by the heels. "That comeback expired days ago."

Seriously though. He's here, right? I'm not imagining some desert oasis of Nico because the shock of the North Carolina chill has been too much to handle and he stopped texting me, right? It's not like I was dying for him or anything, though the urge to run into his arms and lick his neck is hard to fight. I missed his accent, his smile, and his arms and eyes—does he still smell like vanilla and coconuts outside of El Escape?

I can't believe he's here. "You didn't text."

Color hits the apples of his cheeks, and Mom turns the corner, wincing before pasting on her everything-is-rosy face. "Nico arrived a couple of hours ago from New York. Maybe we can go down the street for some din—"

I wave her off. "Wait, what?"

Dad and Mom's grin is Cheshire Cat worthy, and Mom does her excitement bounce.

Nico strides over to the living room couch and grabs my colorful throw pillow. "I, uh, brought you the mate."

Holy ball drop, he did what? "You went to the apartment?" I don't use my kindest tone.

Mom bites both lips between her teeth, and I realize she's curled her hair. She runs her hands down her company-is-coming blouse. They knew about this? I'd yell at them in French, but Nico is fluent. Merde.

Dad nudges her into the kitchen. "We'll check the...liquor cabinet."

Mom scoffs and he shrugs.

The world is spinning again. "Um." I point down the hall with a stiletto. "Room."

He follows, one arm holding the pillow to him like a shield, popping into the kitchen to set down his glass before trudging behind me down the hallway of family photos. "So you really didn't know I was coming?"

"No," I toss over my shoulder. No one tries with me. Not until now. I fight a grin even with my mind in all the directions.

I toss my shoes toward the closet and turn to the bed, then away because Nico and beds go together too well and I can't right now for too many reasons, though Nico and most places go hand in hand. Maybe my room isn't the best idea. Dad's office? Too cluttered. Living room? Not unless we want my parents to witness this conversation and no, we do not. I turn to exit, but Nico fills the doorway, steps in, and closes the door with a click. I lean against my desk and grip the edge. I can't believe he came here.

"I didn't text, because I wanted to see you and was afraid you didn't want to see me. And because you asked me to find you. So..." He places the pillow next to the other and runs a hand over it. "I did. It's bright compared to the apartment." He looks me over and shoves his hands in the pockets of his jeans. "Much like you, Cozi. Are you okay with seeing me?"

"Yes, but why? What? I don't—I'm not..." I take a long breath while Nico's face scrunches. "Please explain, because I can't make the words just yet." I cross my arms.

He takes a step closer. "I was an idiot."

It's a solid start. "Did Ilaria convince you to come here? Ruth?" I won't have him coerced into tracking me down because I get along with the others.

"No," he says. "Though they were...loud about it." He rolls his eyes and raises one side of his lips. "Everyone was loud about it. Ilaria and Xiamara went with me to New York—they claimed for some specialty spa shopping, which I think was the truth for Xia." He gives a one-shoulder shrug. "When we found out you were in North Carolina, they calmed down, but I got impatient. They're still there."

I let my hands drop back to the edge of the desk to keep from grabbing him. He wanted to see me. Followed me. And went to New York. It's almost funny, but not quite yet. Maybe another day. "You met James."

He winces, gravitating toward me. "Mm-hmm." I give a tight laugh, and Nico tilts his head at me. "Is that a problem?"

"No, I'm just..." Confused and rather shocked? James's stinging text message makes way more sense now. I bring my eyes back to Nico's. "Is he okay?"

"Well, he wasn't happy that an unknown man showed up

insisting on seeing you. He was less so when I told him that I wouldn't leave until he gave me your parents' number." He bites his lips together as if he's not telling me everything. "I thought you were going back there because that's the address we had on file and my airport contact wasn't keen on sharing your flight destinations, nor did your travel agent know about the change."

"You talked to Helena?" I tip my head and smirk. He did his homework. He tried.

"I did, and she wants you to call her. She thinks highly of you. Everyone does. Why did you leave early?"

"It's not about you, if that's what you think." Okay, so it was a little. I don't expect him to smile, but his lips twitch up. Am I that obvious? "I thought it would mean something to James if I went back to New York, so I caught an earlier flight here."

"You were right to do that. He wants you to come back." He tips his head at my wincing expression. "I wish I would have caught you before you left."

"It shouldn't have gone on for that long, Nico."

"I know." He steps forward but halts when I wave him off. I'm not ready for his touch yet, even though I thirst for it. "Our security guy is good at finding information that's not public, and I didn't think much of your company's impending closure until you told me you knew who I was. Then I panicked and jumped to the incorrect conclusion about you because—" He crinkles his nose.

I tilt my head and give a sad smile. "Because of what some truly dreadful people did to you in the past."

He nods. "Still, I was wrong to pry like that." He scrunches his face, taking another step toward me. "I have no excuse except that I was worried, untrusting, and completely smitten with you. It was wrong, and even worse to expect ill intent from you, and I'm sorry."

"Smitten, huh?"

"Yeah." He steps closer but not close enough. I crave his hands on me again. "So I wanted to see you again and tell you I acted..." His eyes crinkle at the edges as he considers.

"Like a doof?" I provide with a tight smile.

His eyebrow raises. "Yes. Also, pushing you away was terrible, especially when all I wanted to do was tug you closer." His hand settles next to mine on the desk. The warmth makes my pinkie twitch closer until it brushes his skin. He gives me a slight smile.

"Mm-hmm." Not kissing him may be the hardest thing I've ever done. His perfect lips are right there. Mine belong on them, we know this. "Thank you for telling me about cheeseburgers and your mom...mor."

"Mor," he says, completely different from how I did. "I'll tell you more but—"

Cupping his neck, I pull him to me and lock onto his bottom lip. It takes a split-second before his arms wrap around me and he takes over. Yes, he still smells like Nico. Tastes like him, with a hint of scotch. His warmth rolls over me, and the excitement of him being here sends me into trembles.

"I should have shared," he manages between deep kisses.

"I shouldn't have looked you up," I say in response. "And I should have talked to you before...before Christmas happened."

"No." He shakes his head, brushing his lips back and forth against mine. "There was no way I would have handled that well, but I shouldn't have lashed out. I just spiraled and then when I considered everything..." He tugs at my bottom lip with his teeth, then kisses away the sting. "Everything you are, I knew I ruined what could have been, and I'd never see you again."

Relearning the hard angle of his jaw and the muscles of his shoulder is a decent start to having things feel normal between us again. How odd that he's slipped into my normal so quickly.

"What changed your mind about me?"

He cups my face and tilts my head back to lick my throat into a kiss. "I decided that even if you were like the others..." His lips brush down my neck until he reaches the hollow between my collarbones, making me squirm. "I couldn't stay away from you."

I'd stop him, but he's made it back up to the sensitive place under my ear and I melt, held up only by his arms. "That's fucked up, Nico."

His breath tickles my skin. "I have some issues. But I'm starting to trust. You didn't take things to the tabloids."

"No. No, I didn't, nor would I ever."

He does have issues, and we're going to have to work through them, because I won't have him accusing me all the time because he's scarred from his past. I won't be able to go through this multiple times, and if that's how it's going to be each time he's mad at me, we may as well walk away now.

"I have my own money, and I'll probably have a new job by tomorrow. I don't need you. Not like that."

He grins at me as I trace my fingers over the sweater he's wearing, a little sad for the thick, teasing barrier, as I gather my thoughts about the worst infraction I can imagine.

"I'd never use a baby to trap you," I say, holding his gaze. "I'm serious. Never. Do you have kids?"

Being a quirky stepmom isn't the most terrifying thing. *Slow down, Cozette.*

"No. Not yet." He gives me that soft kiss that makes my insides shudder and melt to goo before he pulls back, holding my face and stroking both cheeks with his thumbs. That tropical blue color slides up to focus on my eyes. His true and real smile makes my chest warm, branching out in hot waves through my limbs. "You're so sweet and I'm not sure anyone has made me laugh like you do." He brushes my hair behind my ear. "I don't know you well enough, but in my soul I know you are good. That was so unique to me, I couldn't believe you were real."

Before I can jump into his arms, he presses his forehead to mine. His fingers skim my back, and I wrap my pant-clad legs around his hips. "Cozi, whatever this is between us needs more time. When you left, all the color drained out of Simona Island, and it left me stumbling through a gray world."

I nod against him and sniffle. It was like that. "I'm warmer now than I've been since you left me."

"God, I'm so sorry." His fingers dig into my hip, and he tightens his grip.

"Don't do it again." I kiss his scruffy jaw, his chin, then his lips.

"I won't. Come work for me."

A turntable screech rips through my mind, and I lean back. "I'm not working for you."

"Why not?" he asks with a smirk.

"This is not a game, Nico. You want me to do the exact thing you condemned me for."

He moves closer, and I palm his chest to halt him.

"I was fighting the truth because I have difficulty getting over my past," he says. "You fit and we need you. You belong at El Escape. And I believe you belong with me too."

That's a convincing argument. I ran away to find myself and instead discovered a place and a person that make me comfortable enough to be me, full throttle. It's been days, and I itch to have the sand under my feet, see another sunrise, swim, explore, work, find even more favorite positions.

Nico grins wide. "Good. That's decided then."

"It's not," I say, finding it difficult not to smile.

"Oh yeah? What's holding you here?" His grip relaxes, and he tugs on my jacket lapels. "You can wear a suit on the island if you want, but it may be odd since shoes are stupid."

My glare is thwarted when he steals a kiss. "I put my résumé out there," I whisper against his lips. "I'll get job offers soon."

"I'll beat their offers."

Ugh. I shove at him, but he doesn't budge. "Absolutely not. You're not buying me, Nico. Yes, I'm good at what I do, but I will not let you hire me just because you want me around. Maybe Vic has something? Or the tree houses?"

"Jose told me that Vic stole you away. We thought you were staying there."

Oh, that's why Jose was so sullen. He thought I wasn't happy with El Escape. Aw. "Nope. I only hitched a ride to the airport. Vic told me a lot about the island though." I poke his chest. "You're secretive, you know that, right?"

He scrunches his nose. "Yes. I won't be secretive with you. Or I'll try not to be. It's a long-standing habit."

That's understandable. "If I know things, I'll be sure to tell you. Like how Vic told me that Angel is the owner of the island."

"Ah. Yeah. Actually…I own the island." He nods at my raised eyebrow expression. "I bought it from Angel a couple of years ago for pennies, but with miles of paperwork on how it's to be treated, not that I'd turn it into a commercial hub or anything. Simona Island is almost perfect."

"Almost?" I ask.

"You're not there yet. Now stop stalling." He taps my nose. "Vic can't have you. You're too playful for The Cliffs, and my staff would show up with pitchforks and steal you back."

His expression asks me to play with him, but I'm not sold. I've known him for days and fell for him, the staff, and location of El Escape—but people fall in love with vacations. What if that wears off?

"I can see the wheels of doubt spinning behind your eyes, Elskede."

"Elskede?"

He bites back a laugh, eyes crinkling at the corners. I don't think my Danish pronunciation is up to par.

"Beloved," he says, like it's a benign, not-staggering term of endearment. As if he said "person" or "door" or "lamp." He thumbs my bottom lip. "Fine. We'll negotiate. I've needed a dedicated events director for a while now. Ilaria and Ruth are pulled in too many directions and will tell you the same."

He lifts me against him, kisses the hell out of me, fingers in my hair. With a growl I'm going to work to recreate later, he sets me on my feet and takes a step back, standing tall with his feet shoulder-width apart and arms at his sides.

His stance brings my attention to three things. His defined shoulders even under a thick sweater, the bulge in his jeans that makes my mouth water, and his determined business face. The latter is new to me, and the part of me that's attracted to powerful businessmen jumps around clapping.

I put my hands on my hips and tilt my chin up. "So, negotiate."

Is this a good idea? He came for me, missed me. There's nowhere else I'd rather be, but I can't lock myself there, or to him. There are too many what-ifs.

"El Escape Azul would like to offer you full-time employment in event and conference management, with a full benefits package, housing, and meals."

I shake my head. "I'm not comfortable accepting a brand-new position that will entwine me for an indeterminable amount of time on a private island in a different country. I *may* consider a contractor position."

His pursed lips hold my attention, as the tension of business games rolls up my spine and makes my ears tingle. It's been a long time since I've stood on this field. I'm tempted to do some of those boxing warm-ups like Madison and Jamal did for the weird talent showdown.

"A year contract position is available with potential for

extension into the aforementioned employee package," he says in a matter-of-fact tone.

I'd be obligated to El Escape for a full year. What if Nico changes his mind? There's no way that if I go back, we're not going to end up in beds and on counters...the floor, any couch in a private space. What would be the downfall if in six months, when I've established events, Nico and I can't make it work? Awkward, and if these last few days are any indication—crushing.

"This is business, Ms. Fay." His jaw clenches. I liked what he called me earlier better. "You are El Escape's ideal candidate for the event team. We need your ability to create unique entertainment opportunities for guests, sometimes on the spot. Even while on vacation, you've proved what you can do."

"Time-out." I form a T with my hands. "Our last spat would have been infinitely worse if I lived there. If whatever is between us fizzles, we're still contractually attached. Can you manage someone you've slept with?"

His cheeks tint pink, and he scrunches his nose. "Time-out accepted. I won't touch on the former yet, but...Xiamara and I about a year ago...it was brief, and we both knew it wasn't what we wanted. We work together fine."

I widen my eyes before slapping my negotiations face on again. Oh. Okay then. "Nico, I can't go through seeing you every day and not being able to touch you if things don't pan out for us." I've known the man a week, and being separated from him ripped me open in a way I've never experienced.

His fingers clench at his sides. "Cozi..." He fixes me with a hard stare. "It's us. To the best of my ability, I won't hurt you again."

It's us.

He's right. Whether it was some Christmas spirit that led me to this fate, or a chance encounter that delivered me into the arms of the person created by my greatest dreams, I'm more positive about a future filled with *us* than I've been about anything besides being an event planner. From the moment we walked out of the airport together, it was *us*.

I swallow hard, fighting the urge to launch myself back into the arms where I belong, but we haven't worked this out yet. Getting a chance to know him for real this time, to date and settle into a new project, is something I want, but binding myself there so soon isn't wise. It's too new. Exciting, but risky. I need a short-term plan.

"Time-out complete," I say, making another T and breaking it, putting my hands back on my hips. "I would consider a one-month contract to determine El Escape Azul's needs and develop a one-year plan of event and conference development."

"Six-month contract to develop a five-year plan and begin implementation."

I purse my lips. There's no way I can leave projects mid-completion. "If I start implementing, the contract will extend."

He smirks. This side of him is exciting. He has a business mind under those swim trunks and teasing lip nibbles. He's already evaluated how I'll react to his pitched angles from our previous conversations, and he's working me to get what he wants too. I try to keep from visibly swooning, but he bites that lip and I'm probably busted.

Maybe I shouldn't fight fair either. I brush my finger over my lips as I pretend to think, then trail them down my neck to flick at the first button on my shirt. His eyes follow my movement, smugness faltering into focused determination.

"Three months compiling a five-year development plan," I say and wet my bottom lip.

Nico takes a step forward, looming over me. I'm a tiny planet facing a burning sun. "Four-month contract. That's three months for assessment and development planning, then one month implementing *or* training another for the position.

Besides...you're going to want to be there for the Moss Monster Meet."

That's a damn good deal. My heart is pounding. "And that's in April?"

"June." Then he does his lip tuck.

I give him a teasing glare but don't call him on his math. "Housing?" I ask. I don't need to ask about salary. Nico may not know it, but if I can stay at El Escape and get paid in sunrises, orgasms, and food from Chef Jules, I'm square.

"You'll have a roommate." His lips twitch.

I shake my head. "No, I won't."

"Mm-hmm. We'll see." He lets a grin slip through his business facade. "You'll have your own quarters until you can't bear to stay away from me in the evenings. We slept well that night, didn't we?"

I crack a smile. "Maybe. I passed out from overexertion."

He makes a fleeting pout. "You'll remember next time. Tonight maybe, after we ring in a new year." He holds up a finger before I respond. "Name your salary."

"Industry standard for this position."

He snorts. "Absolutely not. You're not the industry standard."

"If I don't work over a forty-hour week, I am."

He silently ponders as his gaze trails over my face. It reminds me of how he looked at me the day after Christmas—as if he's studying me, memorizing the moment.

His chest rises and falls. "Cozette Fay, I'd like to offer you a four-month contractor assignment at El Escape Azul. Room and board will be provided by the establishment and work hours capped at forty hours per week. Wages will be fifteen percent over the industry standard." He gives me a look that begs me to fight him on the last part.

I bite at my grin, but it won't stop. "I'll consider it."

Nico nods and runs a hand through his hair. "If El Escape

isn't what you want, I can take a hiatus and move here, though I would have to increase my winter wardrobe significantly." He steps closer, brushing his hand over my hip. "But sunrises wouldn't be the same. Mountains instead of ocean. Leaning against a..." His nose scrunches. "Uh, North Carolina tree instead of a palm trunk."

"Oak maybe?"

"Sure. That. But there's always coffee so..." He shrugs.

The buzz of silliness leaves me at the serious question in his eyes. My throat tightens. He'd leave paradise for me. I shake my head. "I don't want that." How could I take this man from that island? He belongs there and...I do too.

He tugs me closer, wrapping me up and tilting my chin up. "Tell me what you need, and I'll try hard to make it happen."

I stare up at ocean-blue pools. His chest rises and falls in a deep breath as I tangle my fingers in his waves, and I know he feels it too—our sunrise. Up on tiptoes, I brush my lips against his. "I accept the position."

EPILOGUE
XIAMARA

New York City didn't look like this when I ran the marathon three years ago. Christmas lights, sugar sculptures, and man-sized nutcrackers decorate almost every block this New Year's Eve. I can visualize Cozette wandering these crowded streets, singing carols, and spinning in circles.

She has to forgive Nico. We can't head back to Simona without her. The second she walked in the door in his shirt, the staff started scheming, complete with walkie-talkies and code names. In very rare fashion, I joined in on the gossip my fellow island residents use as their pastime. But with Nico and Cozette? I couldn't help myself. They just gravitated to each other, old souls reuniting. On the jet, he told me that was how it felt. He clutched his chest like he could harness the breaking of his heart, and it smacked a place in me that is always present. But I've had seven years to cope with what couldn't be.

Yet that didn't stop me from tagging along. I have good reasons to be here other than supporting Nico, and I've accomplished those—but in a distracted state, because one thing has permeated through my tasks today like a drop of patchouli in a blend of chamomile. Apollo may be here, walking these same streets.

I should thank him for keeping my brain so haywire, because I haven't had time to talk myself out of dropping off essential oil samples at my three favorite New York perfumeries. I snagged three diffuser sticks from each—prizes for my bravery. And now, I have inspiration for a few blends I can use in the spa.

Normally, I'd have taken notes and be going home with hundreds of ideas, but my senses are too busy peeking around each corner, scanning each face, and listening in on passing conversations, as if a passerby would actually say, "Hey, it's Apollo Fischer."

It's not like he's famous or anything—unless you're on Simona Island.

I shouldn't have come. He brings out a side of me I'd love to conquer but haven't a clue how. I study the crowd as if his beautiful face would be swimming in this ocean of parka-covered people. With distance and the years between us, I'd nearly forgotten how absurd I act when he's on my mind.

I need a distraction from these thoughts. Nico checked in hours ago when he arrived at Cozette's parents' house to wait for her to get back from an interview. Mama hit up a show because I wouldn't let her come with me, knowing we'd end up shopping instead. I pull off a glove with my teeth and text our group chat. *Well?* That's all I manage to type because brr. I slide my phone away and peek around another corner, straight down car-packed Lexington Avenue.

This is silly. I'm an adult. I've completed marathons, won the island's Moss Monster Meet twice and will do it again this year so I can take the Moss Boss title from Mama. She's kept the shell trophy for two decades for winning the Mossy three times, and she also holds the best record for the drink tray dash in the thirty-six years Simona has held the competition. That may be my most successful event out of the five because I was carrying a tray to help at the hotel when I was knee high. The wave rescue event will be a beast, followed by the loaded golf cart tour, but I'll fly through the waterfall wedding ring retrieval and the lost tourist jungle hunt.

A taxi's beep coincides with a stranger's irritated huff at my reluctance to make my way across the massive intersection, and I pick up the pace, hitting a stride that rivals rushing native New Yorkers.

How many times has Apollo walked these streets in the last seven years? Does he scan faces when he sneaks into Simona and hope to see mine—or hope not to?

I power walk myself into the entrance of the hotel and slam to a halt. A man stands in the lobby facing away from me. He's black with short hair, and he has on a blue suit. Correct build, correct height. Oh god. I'm five feet from him and my stomach sinks, every bit of moisture in my mouth evaporating. Heat floods my cheeks as he shifts, rocks, slowly turns, and...

It's not Apollo.

This man is handsome, but his eyes aren't the color of honey and his skin isn't sun-kissed bronze. His lips don't do that slight delay on the left side when Apollo smiles.

Scooting around him, I hide myself in the back corner of the lobby in a chair that is far more stylish than comfortable and pull out my phone again. Only one person can talk some sense into me, because she's never met Apollo and therefore has no preconceived notions, and she won't tell me not to act this way.

"I'm peeing in a public restroom right now so deal with it," Roxanne says instead of hello. I'm not sure she's ever answered with a common greeting. "Hadley's at her dad's so we can speak freely. Fucking hi."

My laugh echoes in the streamlined lobby as I sink into the

hard angles of the chair, ignoring the raised eyebrow of the desk attendant. "You could have called me back, because ew."

"Please. Half of your job is massage therapy. Like you're unfamiliar with bodily functions."

"Okay, one point to you. But you could have waited. It's not that important." It is though. I'm losing my mind here. The toilet flushes, and despite my stress, I smile.

"I had to answer. I want details. Did you all save love or what?"

"Don't know yet. But I'm having a freak-out moment."

She gives a light hiss through the line, and water turns on. "You haven't run into him, have you?"

"This is why I love you. I didn't even tell you why I'm freaking out, but you always know."

Roxanne laughs and a door opens, unleashing a crowd before it's silenced by another slam. "I'm outside now. That should be better. You don't freak out often, sugar tush, but you're in NYC and if anyone would have called you back yet about your sample packs, you'd be in full wackadoodle mode. So explain."

She's one of the few who knows the true story of Apollo and me. How we were best friends until he confessed wanting more. How it wasn't a one-sided attraction, but my fear of ruining our friendship threw me off my axis. How among all the things that I fumbled, the worst first kiss in the history of kisses sealed our fate. We tried, we failed, we moved on.

I tell her about my day, the places I went, how I see glimpses of him everywhere.

"I don't know, Xia. Maybe it's one of your universe signs."

"What do you mean?"

"Not to freak you out further or anything, but you have a pretty keen sense of him. Like that time you knew he was on the island, but no one said he was on the island."

"Yeah, that was weird." I thought I was losing my mind.

Mama, the gossip pulse of Simona, let it slip that he was visiting. I didn't sleep for two nights and finally broke, determined to go to The Cliffs to see him, but got as far as my golf cart, head on the steering wheel. I just can't physically function around the man.

My phone buzzes. I tell Roxanne to hang on and check the screen. It's Nico. *Cozette is coming to Simona Island. We have four months to convince her to stay forever.*

I grin wide and send him a party-face emoji and ten hearts.

"Good news," I say, bringing the phone back up to my ear. "We have a new Simona Island resident. Nico says Cozette's trying out Simona for four months."

Roxanne laughs. "*Trying out.* That's sweet. It's painful leaving every time I visit you for the Mossy, and hey, since we're on the topic of the one-kiss-wonder plus a brave move in the name of love...maybe you should reach out to Apollo."

"I can't, Rox, and you know it."

She sighs right into the phone, most likely on purpose. "Then let him go, woman. You can't live your life walking around with wishful Apollo mirages all over the place."

"I moved on long ago."

"Oh, honey." She tuts. "You won't have a relationship, and you're not enjoying New York. The only things you do for yourself are cooking up smells—though that's often to benefit others—and winning the Mossy. Humor me. Let's go through some scenarios. What if he's married and has kids?"

My stomach does a series of acrobatics and kicks the air out of my lungs.

"I'm going to take your silence as a Xia freak-out moment and let that one slide. Next, what if he returned to Simona?"

I open my satchel and fidget with the ends of the diffuser sticks. "He returns to see his mom and sister."

"No, like—" She drops her voice to a deep tone. "*I'll be back for you, Xiamara Nivar.*"

"That's not what he said."

We hadn't spoken for four months, the longest we'd gone without seeing each other since we were kids. He was headed to New York for college, while I was headed to Florida. He'd come to say goodbye and cornered me in my room, cupped my face, and set his forehead against mine. "I'm coming back after graduation," he said. "Don't make me wait too long, Xiamara Nivar. This island is in our blood, and we belong here. Together."

I returned four years later. He did not. Not that I cared. He had a case of puppy love, or small island syndrome, and was cured of it by this big city and all the people who were not me.

Roxanne clears her throat. "Xia?"

I swallow a different kind of emotion. "He was a kid then."

"He was almost an adult and so were you. I don't like that you have regrets. Now really, what would you do if he came back?" Great. Roxanne's switched to her mom voice. She means business.

"I'd need to learn to act like a normal person around him so I don't embarrass myself in front of all the residents of Simona. I live there."

There's a soft laugh through the line. "You and your pride."

"I'm not proud," I say, then crinkle my nose. "That sounded weird. I'm not—"

"You don't want the people you love to see you as less than perfect. It's pride, Xia. Though I've seen you in a ton of compromising positions, so where does that put me?"

"Uh, in best friend position, obviously. I didn't meet you until college, it's different. I just…you don't know what it's like to grow up in a tiny town where everyone knows your business."

"That is true. I was one in a million in Philly. Okay, so what would happen if Apollo returned and professed his love for you to the entire island?"

"I'd come live with you." The words pop out from some mini-brain that thinks much faster than my actual brain understands.

"You're such a weirdo. Oh! What if he came back to the island and joined the Moss Monster Meet? I believe you've said that was a life goal for both of you."

It was. Simona kids grow up diving for parents' rings in the bathtub, pretending they're in the deep pool under the waterfalls and racing over hot sand carrying rocks on chunks of bark as our tray of drinks and food. Apollo left without competing once.

"One," I say, holding a finger in the air like she's in front of me, "he'd have to work on the island, and he doesn't. And two, I'm winning the Mossy."

Thank you for reading! Did you enjoy? Please add your review because nothing helps an author more and encourages readers to take a chance on a book than a review.

Don't miss more from Poppy Minnix with the next book in the Simona Island series coming soon, and discover her paranormal stories at www.poppyminnix.com

Want more holiday goodness? Check out EIGHT DAYS OF CHRISTMAS, by City Owl Author, Starla DeKruyf. Turn the page for a sneak peek!

You can also sign up for the City Owl Press newsletter to receive notice of all book releases!

SNEAK PEEK OF EIGHT DAYS OF CHRISTMAS
BY STARLA DEKRUYF

Isabella Whitley gripped both armrests and prayed she wouldn't die in a fiery plummet to the earth. Only clouds filled the view out the plane's window, but the aircraft jolted sideways and up and down, so vigorously that she closed her eyes and did the most ridiculous thing given her situation.

She *laughed*.

The irony of the moment was almost as painful as it was comical. Because wasn't this what her life had become now? A life in complete disarray and full of turbulence?

Bob—the complete stranger in the seat next to Isabella who'd talked non-stop since the wheels lifted from the JFK runway—cleared his throat. "I-it's going to be okay. We-we're going to be fine. Promise."

Isabella rolled her eyes and glanced down at his fisted hands in his lap, his knuckles white. What did Bob know? How did he know everything would be okay? And why was he so positive anyway? He'd already confessed that his girlfriend had dumped him, moved out and taken their cat with her, and his father died after choking on a shrimp—all in the last few weeks.

The plane rocked angrily, and Isabella inhaled a sharp breath. Sure, her life currently sucked, maybe not as bad as Bob's, but she definitely didn't want to die by way of a plane crash.

"H-hey, you've been letting me talk your ear off," Bob

mumbled. "Besides your name, I don't know anything about you. How 'bout you tell me about yourself?"

Isabella didn't open up to just anyone. And on an airplane headed back home for the first time in ten years definitely wouldn't be one of those times. People often mistook this as a sign that she was a good listener—people other than her ex-boyfriend, Harrison Blake, anyway.

Harrison used this as one of the reasons to end their relationship. His exact words had been: *It's like you've built a wall around your heart, and after four years, it's still impossible to get in. Someone broke your heart. Broke you. And I can't help you. If you ever want me to commit, you gotta figure this out.*

Technically, their relationship hadn't ended. Harrison asked her to move out of his modern apartment and suggested they *take a break*. But who really knew what that meant? Was this a Ross and Rachel break? Or were they free to see other people?

As the floor beneath her feet continued to rumble, Isabella found herself asking, "What do you wanna know, Bob?" If she did die today, she refused to prove Harrison right.

"So, you live in New York?"

She nodded, picturing Central Park, and took a calming breath.

"And w-what do you do for a living?"

"I'm a journalist. At *The New Yorker*."

Bob exhaled a low whistle. "Impressive."

Gah, had she said too much? She tried not to be paranoid, but with her career, she'd met an unsuspecting creep or two in her day. The few things Bob knew about her could be enough for him to locate any of her social media profiles or find her bio on *The New Yorker*'s website for that matter. From there it would only be a matter of time before he had her address.

Except as of now, she technically didn't have a home address. The thought of Bob showing up at Harrison's apartment provoked the bubble of a laugh in her throat. *Joke's on you Bob.* She didn't live there anymore.

Something inside her withered. Not having an address linked to her name was the opposite of funny—it was disturbing and downright pathetic. She'd worked tirelessly to reach her current position at *The New Yorker* and what did she have to show for it? A new popcorn maker she'd left at Harrison's apartment and a strict wardrobe of blazers and designer boots.

Since living in Manhattan for the past ten years, she'd relied on city transit and subways, so she didn't even have a car. She didn't own a single thing with her name attached to it. Currently, Isabella was crashing on Margo and Todd's old, lumpy couch. Her friends from college had a two-bedroom apartment with each of them occupying a room.

She wasn't complaining. She was grateful for a place to stay, even if it was a slightly dilapidated apartment building just outside of the city, while Harrison's modern and recently renovated building was in the heart of NYC.

Isabella couldn't dwell on the issue of technically being homeless, which was how she knew Dad would label it.

Dad. She probably missed him the most. He'd been so supportive and encouraged her to follow her dreams and attend Ithaca College. But when fate threw a wrench into Isabella's plans and she never returned after graduation, he'd been the most resentful toward her.

Scratch that—second most resentful. She'd have to wait to figure out a more permanent living situation after she returned to New York. Right now, her only focus was surviving the next eight days.

The aircraft rattled and Isabella clutched the armrests again. A baby cried somewhere toward the back of the plane.

Bob patted her shoulder. "Everything's gonna be alright."

His stale coffee breath emitted across the small space between them. "Tell me why you're headed to Colorado?"

The plane leveled and Isabella exhaled a breath through her nose. She wasn't typically a nervous flyer. She flew often for work. But a lot was riding on this trip to Colorado. Her family was counting on her—Norah was counting on her.

Maybe by her opening up to Bob, she'd be on her way to proving Harrison wrong. She didn't *always* need to be one of those tough nuts to crack; she could be chatty and charismatic like Norah.

"My sister is getting married," she said. To little Landon Hoffman from next door. Isabella was still trying to swallow that news.

"That's nice. Good reason to travel at Christmas. Unlike me, who has to attend a big pharmaceutical conference..." Bob rambled on.

When Isabella had agreed to be Norah's maid of honor, she had no clue Norah had chosen the week of Christmas to get married. If she'd known, she might've said no. It was almost like Norah chose a Christmas Day wedding on purpose. That way Isabella would be forced to return to Pineridge, not only to celebrate her only sister's new marriage, but to endure the holiday as well, including Eight Days of Christmas—a Whitley tradition where they performed a specific holiday activity each day for eight days leading up to December twenty-fifth.

Norah had left Isabella no choice but to return home and withstand the eleven million questions from her family. No choice but to face Landon's older brother Leo—the boy who held the key to her heart for more years than she could count.

She glanced out the window. Ready or not—she was headed home.

Or maybe not.

Static blared through the plane's overhead speakers, followed by an announcement.

"Good afternoon flight 434, this is your captain speaking. I'm afraid I have some less than exciting news. Due to the snowstorm Denver is currently experiencing, ground control has directed us to make an emergency landing in Omaha, Nebraska."

"What?" Isabella flung herself forward in her seat as groans, disapproving comments, and moans echoed through the cabin. "Is he for real?"

"I'm 'fraid so." Bob gave her a soft smile.

"At any rate," the captain continued, "the good folks at American Airlines customer service will be more than happy to assist you with accommodations. Hopefully the ice and fog will let up in Denver so we can get you all on your way real soon. American Airlines thanks you for flying with us and, as always, don't forget to fill out a customer service survey online and give us a top-star rating."

Just how in the hell was she supposed to make it home now? The plane descended quickly, giving Isabella that queasy feeling in her stomach she despised. This was seriously happening. The pilot was actually landing the plane in Omaha, Nebraska.

"This can't be happening." Isabella closed her eyes, pinching the bridge of her nose.

"Omaha, huh?" Bob said. "Never been here before." He pulled his phone from the front pocket of his laptop bag, ready for when he'd have service. "Better check Yelp for the best places to find some grub."

As if this little emergency pit stop was the best thing to happen to him. Then again, maybe it was.

All around her, phones chimed, signaling service. She exhaled a few deep breaths before slipping her phone from her purse. She pushed her hair behind her ear and scrolled through her notifications. There was a missed call from Dad, a missed call from Norah, and several unanswered texts from

Margo and Norah. But the text that stood out the most was from Harrison.

Harrison: Did you want the Pampered Chef cheese grater? Or the popcorn air popper? I know how much you love popcorn. But I did buy it.

Isabella's eyes burned. She squeezed them tight enough to see floating black spots behind her lids. He was really doing this now? He had some nerve. Dividing their things the week before Christmas? When she wasn't even in town?

Even though he'd sent the text two hours before, Isabella opened her eyes and tapped out a reply.

Isabella: Keep them both.

Isabella: On second thought, no. If you can't wait until I'm back to divide our things, then I want them.

She inhaled a deep breath, holding it in.

Isabella: I didn't know we'd made a decision yet. To divide our things. To be completely over.

She didn't expect a reply, at least not so soon. But regardless, it came.

Harrison: Just figured it would be easier this way.

Isabella: You mean easier for you.

Harrison: Why make it harder than it has to be?

Isabella: After four years together, breaking up shouldn't be easy.

No response—no surprise.

Isabella sent a quick text to Dad to let him know about the flight's detour to Omaha, and to assure Norah everything was fine and not to worry. She'd figure something out.

Eppley Airfield was fully decked out for the holidays. Garland dangled above wide windows, and glimmering lights wrapped around fake trees that lined the walls. All it did was cause a tight pressure in Isabella's chest. By the time she—along with her rolling suitcase and overstuffed carry-on—made it to the customer service for American Airlines, there was already a long line.

"Well, would you look at that line," Bob said, hot on her heels.

"Right?" Isabella huffed. "This is going to take forever."

"Why don't you come with me to get a bite to eat and then we can make our way to customer service afterward."

Isabella glared at him. "I don't have time to get a bite to eat. I have to get on another plane. And fast." In truth, missing the first few days of Eight Days of Christmas sounded amazing, but Isabella's family already saw her as the daughter and sister who abandoned them. Storm or no storm, she had to make it home within the next twenty-four hours.

"Whoa, okay." Bob put up his hands. "I'm sure you'll get on another plane. But not anytime soon. You heard the captain. There's a winter storm rolling through Denver. It's probably gonna be a while. Maybe not even until tomorrow."

Isabella grunted. She rubbed at the tension building between her eyes. She didn't have time for Bob and his rational thinking. Or this line. Or to be in the Omaha airport at all. "You go ahead. I'm gonna wait."

"Alright, alright. I think I might just do that." He backed up, and Isabella exhaled her relief. "Check you later, Miss Bella." He tipped an imaginary hat at her.

"It's *Isa*bella," she said flatly as he, thankfully, walked away. Despite it being Isabella's unlucky day, the customer service line for American Airlines moved swiftly. When it was her turn, she stepped up to the counter and held her head high. She needed to put on her game face. The one she used in the office. The one she used to get the story. The friendly-but-don't-mess-with-me face.

"Good afternoon, welcome to American Airlines. How can I help you today?" The customer service representative—Ben, his name tag read—had too big of a smile plastered on his face for how distraught Isabella felt.

"Hi there. My name is Isabella Whitley. I was on flight 434

en route to Denver, Colorado, but we were rerouted here due to the snowstorm. The reader board," she pointed above Ben's head, "shows all flights to Denver are canceled. But are you sure the info has been updated? Because I need to get on the first available flight. Please."

"I do apologize, ma'am. But as you just said, all flights to Denver have been canceled."

She gritted her teeth, resisting the urge to raise her voice. Ben was only doing his job, but desperation tingled through her unforgivingly.

"Right. I understand that. But when will the next one take off? I need to get on that flight."

"Again, I do apologize. However, I'm unable to give you that info."

She exhaled. "And why not?"

"Because I'm unable to see the future." His smile turned into a smirk.

Isabella recognized a smirk when she saw one. And he was definitely smirking at her now.

She narrowed her eyes and leaned across the counter. "I have to get to Denver. Today. Whatever you need to do to make that happen, *Ben*, do it." She forced out a strangled, "Please."

"Since it's already late afternoon, what I *can* do for you, ma'am, is give you a hotel voucher and hopefully we can get you on a flight tomorrow morning."

She leaned in closer, heat crawling up her neck and spreading into her cheeks. "I don't *want* a hotel voucher. I *want* on a plane."

He rearranged his expression into a jackass blank stare, as if looking straight through her. "Like I said, let me get you that hotel voucher and—"

Isabella slapped her hand on the counter. "Ben, I'd like to speak to your manager."

"Izzy?"

Isabella sucked in a breath. Her back went rigid while her stomach plummeted to the floor. "Oh please, oh please, oh please, no."

She turned around, slowly.

But nope, luck was still not on her side today. Because when she turned, she knew exactly who would be standing there. Not only because his voice was as familiar as her own skin, but because he'd called her *Izzy*. Besides her family, only one other person in this world called her by that childhood nickname.

Leo Hoffman.

"What the hell are you doing?" Leo stood in the customer service line a few patrons back, hands stuffed in the pockets of his black peacoat.

She swallowed, uncertain if she could find her voice to reply. "Leo?"

She had to still be asleep on the plane, having a nightmare. There was no possible way her luck was this bad.

"You think yelling at customer service is actually gonna get you to Colorado faster? Man, you haven't changed a bit." His face, while the same, was older, all sharp lines and dark brown scruff. And too beautiful to even be fair.

She could wake up now. Any minute.

"I just thought...I was just hoping...I," she mumbled, her mouth going dry. This was real, and she sounded like a blubbering idiot instead of the accomplished woman she'd grown up to be. His words registered. "Wait. Haven't changed a bit? What is that supposed to mean?" She glared. "And what are you doing here?"

"What does it look like?" he snapped.

Her brows pinched together. "You're flying somewhere?"

The Leo she knew never left Pineridge.

His gaze shifted to the people who had their attention

trained on the two of them. "Just take your hotel voucher, Izzy. You're holding up the line."

Isabella reluctantly faced Ben and forced a smile, her heart raging against her chest. After all the ways she'd thought about avoiding her ex once she arrived in Pineridge, he was here. In freaking Omaha, Nebraska. With her.

"Look," she said to Ben. "I'm sorry. I know you're just trying to do your job. But you don't understand. I need to get home to Colorado today." She pushed back her unexpected emotions and cleared her throat, feeling the bizarre urge to open up to this guy and win him over. "My little sister is getting married on Christmas Day and—"

"That's still a week away, ma'am. I can guarantee you'll be there by then."

"But you see, my family has this tradition…" She pinched the bridge of her nose, her back absorbing the scrutiny from the other fliers. "They call it Eight Days of Christmas. They expect me to be there." She leaned forward and whispered, "I haven't been home for Christmas in ten years."

And the stupidly handsome ghost of her past had clearly appeared to remind her of that fact.

Ben inhaled a sharp breath. "Ten years? What kind of person doesn't go home for Christmas for ten years?"

Isabella's jaw dropped, and her first instinct was to give in to the fantasy of clutching the navy-blue tie around his neck and choking him with it. But she couldn't be angry with Ben, because he was exactly right. What kind of person didn't go home for Christmas for ten years? What kind of selfish person did that?

Her—that's who.

"Damn it." Leo groaned, now suddenly standing at her side, sporting that sexy, scruffy beard. "What are you gonna do, tell him your life story? It's a little late to get sympathy when you've already pissed someone off." He leaned over the counter, his phone in his hand. "Excuse me, Ben? Where's the airport's car rental located?"

Ben proceeded to give Leo directions while Isabella remained quiet, trying hard to be annoyed with him while also admiring his broad shoulders and obvious fit physique. He smelled good, too, like pine and citrus, and all man and... Jeez, this was a really bad scenario.

Leo took a few steps sideways, hiking a duffel bag over his shoulder. "You can either come with me and rent yourself a car and drive to Pineridge, or you can stay here and harass this nice guy and embarrass yourself further." He held up a palm. "Your choice."

"Whoa, hold on a sec." She shuffled next to him, getting out of the customer service line. "How far is it from here to Pineridge?" Isabella hadn't driven a car since she moved to New York. The thought of driving, especially through a snowstorm, caused her stomach to flip-flop.

"About six hundred miles."

She gasped. "Six hundred miles?"

Leo blew out an exaggerated and annoyed breath. "Yep. And you might want to hurry. Before all of the cars are gone." Leo stalked away from her, his attention fixed on his phone.

Isabella stood there stupefied, staring after the man who had once been her everything.

Pressing her lips together in a grimace, her mind battled over her options: remain stranded in the airport alone or chase after Leo and somehow persuade him to let her catch a ride with him.

With the flight information screens displaying *cancelled* for nearly every departure, her chest tightened while imagining driving through a death-inducing blizzard. In the end, the panic won.

She bit the inside of her cheek, gripped the handle of her rolling suitcase, and stomped off after Leo.

Don't stop now. Keep reading with your copy of EIGHT DAYS OF CHRISTMAS, by City Owl Author, Starla DeKruyf.

And find more from Poppy Minnix at
www.poppyminnix.com

Don't miss more from Poppy Minnix with the next book in the Simona Island series coming soon, and discover her paranormal stories at www.poppyminnix.com

Want more holiday goodness? Check out EIGHT DAYS OF CHRISTMAS, by City Owl Author, Starla DeKruyf!

Holiday magic? Check.
Swoon worthy romance? Check.
Complications of epic proportions? Check.

Ready or not, Isabella Whitley is returning to her snowy hometown of Pineridge, Colorado for her sister's Christmas wedding. She wants in and out unscathed. Unlikely. A decade ago, she headed to New York and hasn't looked back. Now she must explain her disappearing act to not only her family, but the high-school sweetheart she left behind as well.

Enter Leo Hoffman. He's frosty after striving—and failing—to forget Isabella, the only woman capable of jingling his bells. Since his brother is marrying her sister, Leo is forced to celebrate Eight Days of Christmas with Isabella and her family —a tradition where they perform a different holiday activity each day leading up to December 25th.

Soon, their close proximity brings back memories—and the inability to keep their hands off one another. There's only one problem. Isabella's ex unexpectedly enters the equation, and she faces a difficult choice. Listen to her heart or her head? Isabella will need to decide, once and for all, where she belongs.

Please sign up for the City Owl Press newsletter for chances to win special subscriber-only contests and giveaways as well as receiving information on upcoming releases and special excerpts.

All reviews are **welcome** and **appreciated**. Please consider leaving one on your favorite social media and book buying sites.

Escape Your World. Get Lost in Ours! City Owl Press at www.cityowlpress.com.

ACKNOWLEDGMENTS

Mom and Dad, you always made sure holidays were full of love and celebrated thoroughly. When you reverted to joyful kids again, I noticed. Thank you for those memories.

To the lovely, enthusiastic, intelligent women of the best writer's group ever; you all push me higher every day, whether with emoji faces on last line shares, brainstorming, or conversations on hard subjects in the writing world. I appreciate the fa-la-la out of you and also the critiquers and beta readers who helped polish Holiday Hotel to its glitter-shiny state by pointing out things that didn't line up, my poor French translations, and how much they enjoyed certain Christmas curses.

To my hub's amazing family—your support of creative endeavors is stunning. Thank you for reaching out, asking about all my works in progress, buying my book, and telling me how proud you are of me. I wish every creator had you in their lives.

Mary! You've been an absolute joy to work with. Thank you for your incredible edits, brilliant guidance, and helping nail down sentences I didn't know what to do with. (I'm side-eyeing you, first line). Huge thanks as well to polishing pro René who went above and beyond on copy edits.

The entire City Owl team is top-notch. You not only provide a phenomenal product, but a comfortable, loving environment for your authors. I appreciate you all and your amazing authors! Hugs and hoots to them too! Having a support system like this wasn't something I expected. You're talented, kind, helpful, and I'm so happy to be part of the flock with you.

ABOUT THE AUTHOR

One bleary winter, Poppy Minnix accidentally wrote a novel—a paranormal romance she obsessively typed out in five weeks. Years later, she still barely sleeps, has nightmares of exploding biscuit cans when she does (it's a valid phobia!), and writes every waking minute.

She lives in Maryland with a husband who is far more romantic than she is and two delightful kids who kindly open the terrifying dough bombs for her. They are all kept busy by the best rescue lab-ish mongrel ever, and two cats who think they are dogs.

Along with authoring, she's also the co-host of Punch Keys Podcast, an encouraging podcast for navigating the writing world.

www.poppyminnix.com

twitter.com/PoppyMinnix
instagram.com/poppyminnix
facebook.com/poppymwrites
goodreads.com/poppyminnix

ABOUT THE PUBLISHER

City Owl Press is a cutting edge indie publishing company, bringing the world of romance and speculative fiction to discerning readers.

Escape Your World. Get Lost in Ours!

www.cityowlpress.com

facebook.com/YourCityOwlPress
twitter.com/cityowlpress
instagram.com/cityowlbooks
pinterest.com/cityowlpress

Made in the USA
Middletown, DE
17 April 2024